SLUM ONLINE

HIROSHI SAKURAZAKA

SLUM ONLINE

HIROSHI SAKURAZAKA

TRANSLATED BY JOSEPH REEDER

HAIKA SORU

SAN FRANCISCO

Slum Online
© 2005 Hiroshi Sakurazaka
Originally published in Japan by Hayakawa Publishing, Inc.

Bonus Round
© 2010 Hiroshi Sakurazaka, originally written for Slum Online Haikasoru edition.

English translation by Joseph Reeder
Cover illustration by toi8

Published by
VIZ Media, LLC
295 Bay Street
San Francisco, CA 94133

www.haikasoru.com

Sakurazaka, Hiroshi, 1970-
  [Suramu onrain. English]
  Slum online / Hiroshi Sakurazaka ; translated by Joseph Reeder.
      p. cm.
  "Originally published as: "Suramu onrain" in Japan by Hayakawa Shobo, 2005."
  ISBN 978-1-4215-3439-8
  I. Reeder, Joseph. II. Title.
  PL875.5.A45S8713 2010
  895.6'36--dc22
                                        2009051092

The rights of the author of the work in this publication to be so identified have been asserted in accordance with the Copyright, Designs and Patents Act 1988. A CIP catalogue record for this book is available from the British Library.

Printed in the U.S.A.

First printing, April 2010

> CONTENTS

/ END

I PRESSED THE Ⓐ BUTTON and was no longer Etsuro Sakagami.

I had become Tetsuo.

Music spilled from the speakers. I sat before a twenty-five-inch tube television, three cables snaking from inputs on the front of the set to a game console lying on the floor, a joystick held lightly in my fingers. Two more cords ran between the console and the wall, one to an electrical outlet and the other to a LAN jack.

My room was typical, nothing fancy. Shelves and racks lined the walls, filled to bursting with paperback novels, DVDs, and video games. Wires threaded their way between the piles of junk that littered the floor. I had a dresser, but most of my clothes were on hangers suspended from the curtain rail. Outside my room, an ordinary hallway led to a flight of steep stairs, and beyond that an ordinary living room. All part of an ordinary house in an ordinary neighborhood. This particular ordinary house belonged to my parents, and I called it home.

A motorbike *putt-putt-putted* down the road that ran past our house. A police car trailed close behind, orders to pull over crackling loudly over the bullhorn mounted on its roof. Beneath the road, a fat fiber optic cable had been laid through gas company-owned pipe space in the ground. The signal created when I pressed the A button was traveling through that cable right now, a compressed packet of data moving at the speed of light—300,000 kilometers per second in a vacuum, fast enough to circle the earth seven and a half times in the span of a second. The packet raced south beneath the asphalt, flying past the motorbike as it plodded along at a leisurely 36 kph.

A busy ramen shop stood on the street corner. Illegally parked cars lined the shoulder of the road near the shop, much as they did every night. A middle-aged man squatted beneath a light pole at the side of the road, vomiting up a partially digested broth of beer and noodles. A woman standing in line outside the shop, her brow knitted in disgust, shielded herself behind her boyfriend. Across the intersection a foreigner was robbing the clerk of a twenty-four-hour convenience store at knifepoint. Oblivious to the crime unfolding a stone's throw away, the police continued barking orders for the motorbike to pull over, the staticky pop of their voices echoing through the humid night air. Rows of red taillights trailed off into the distance.

The packet left all that behind as it hurtled toward the hub that would guide it on its way. No sooner had the A button signal passed through a series of computers and reached the server than it turned back into a packet racing down the same fiber optic network it had just traversed. Past *Gimme all your money!* Past *Stop the bike now!* Past *Ew, gross!* Then into the house, across the living room, up the stairs, down the hall, into my room and through the LAN cable stretched across the floor.

Tetsuo sprang to life.

The television screen displayed an aerial view that looked down on Tetsuo at a 45-degree angle. He wore a short school uniform with pants that looked like an old pair of bellbottoms. A white headband held back his spiky manga hair. On his feet were a pair of high wooden clogs. No socks.

The fingers of my right hand rested on the controller's three buttons while my left held the stick with a light yet steady grip, the way a cook might hold an egg. Pressing the stick to the right would move Tetsuo forward toward the middle of the screen, left would move him backwards. The A button made him block, the B button punch, and the C button kick. Combinations of stick movements and button presses could make Tetsuo perform a variety of complex maneuvers.

I tapped the stick twice to the right and Tetsuo broke into a run. A wall of cel-shaded polygonal blocks scrolled by in perfect sync with Tetsuo's stride. A polygonal road glided beneath his feet. Polygonal furniture set in polygonal houses peeked out from behind digital glass. A pair of too-perfect clouds like butter rolls drifted in the unreal turquoise blue sky. Light poles cast unchanging shadows on the ground, the sharp angles of their underlying wireframe almost, but not quite, concealed. Just another sunny day in Versus Town.

Tetsuo ran down the broad Main Street that cut through the center of town. In front of him a landscape of grainy pixels winked into life only to snuff out just as quickly in his wake.

It may have been eleven o'clock at night, but Versus Town was just waking up. There were other people on the street with Tetsuo, all of them running along the right side of the road. Not a one was standing or walking at a regular pace.

Tetsuo rounded a corner. He hopped a wall and then turned another corner. A man was coming straight toward Tetsuo along the left side of the road.

I pressed the A button to stop. My fingers tilted the stick, commanding Tetsuo forward and to the left. A fraction of a second later, Tetsuo responded by planting a foot and veering leftward. Tetsuo and the man brushed against each other, each spinning around the point of impact. If I hadn't stepped to the side when I did, they would have collided head-on.

I pulled out my keyboard and started hammering, my words appearing in a bubble over Tetsuo's head as I typed.

> Watch where you're going!

Judging by his fighting stance, the man standing before Tetsuo was a capoeirista, and a heavyweight at that. He stood a full head taller than the middleweight Tetsuo, and the capoeirista had the bulk to match the height. The capoeirista remained silent. Unsatisfied, I continued my tirade of text.

> Ever hear of walking on the right side of the road?

He wore a camouflage-textured tank top and a red wristband wrapped tightly around his right arm. Tetsuo put his hands on his hips in a gesture of frustration.

> Helloooo? Anybody home?

The capoeirista answered with a kick.

There was no way to see it coming. Like a frog staring at an unsuspecting fly before flicking out its tongue, the capoeirista's expression never changed. No feelings manifested on that polygonal face to betray his thoughts.

Defenseless, Tetsuo took the full brunt of the capoeirista's sweeping kick. The force of the blow sent him flying. Spinning as he sailed through the air, Tetsuo slammed into a nearby wall and fell crashing to the ground. A meaty, exaggerated thud burst from the speakers. Crack details marred the concrete blocks at the point of impact. Tetsuo's health gauge fell by 10 percent.

Text bubbled over the capoeirista's head.

> Shut up, karateka.

I adjusted my grip on the stick. My hands blurred over the controls. Tetsuo vaulted off the ground with a kip-up, putting some distance between himself and the capoeirista. The capoeirista charged, unleashing a forward kick as Tetsuo got to his feet. I didn't bother with the A button. Using only the stick, I maneuvered Tetsuo back and to the left, sidestepping the attack. The capoeirista was already well into his next move.

Capoeira is a traditional martial art from Brazil that makes extensive use of foot techniques. Their kicks and sweeps trace graceful arcs that make the fighter look half a dancer in battle.

But behind those kicks lurks deadly strength, especially when delivered with the force of a heavyweight.

A low sweep. A torso kick. An axe kick. A step-in round-house. The capoeirista left no gap between his attacks, putting Tetsuo solidly on the defensive. When the barrage finally ended there was a brief, but significant, recovery time before the capoeirista could move again. Heavyweights packed a lot of power in each attack, but they took longer to recover too, leaving them vulnerable. That was the price they paid for their raw power.

I timed a flying knee to land after his next lunge. Tetsuo's knee made contact with a satisfying *thunk* that signaled a successful counterhit, and the capoeirista soared. I kneed his body once more in the air and then crouched to meet him with a punch as he landed. Before the punch animation had even finished, I was already inputting my next command: two quick taps on the stick. The instant the cooldown from his last attack ended, Tetsuo dashed forward. Pressing the A button to cancel out of the run, I followed up with a low foot sweep. Tetsuo dashed again and brought a punch crashing down squarely onto the fallen capoeirista's back. As his opponent rose to his feet, Tetsuo jabbed with his fastest punch. Now the capoeirista was playing defense.

I canceled out of a punch-kick combo and tapped the command to speed-dash. Tetsuo retracted his right leg midswing and darted forward. *Time for a throw.* Tetsuo grabbed the capoeirista by the scruff of the neck and hammered him with a head butt that sent him sprawling on his back. Tetsuo moved after him so quickly he might have been the heavyweight's shadow.

The capoeirista rolled to one side, sweeping out with his leg as he regained his feet. It was the textbook response, and I'd seen it coming a mile away. Tetsuo dodged the attack with ease before firing another knee strike. It connected with a mighty crunch. Tetsuo snuck in another knee as the capoeirista hung suspended in the air, and the heavyweight went flying into the wall.

I punched the capoeirista as his body rebounded. *Cancel, punch. Punch, kick, cancel, heel drop. Crouching punch. Speed dash. Cancel. Low foot sweep.* When it was over, the crumpled ruin of Tetsuo's opponent lay on the ground, motionless. A moment later, he vanished from the screen. My hands moved to the keyboard.

> Out of your league, scrub.

~

Versus Town existed online, its only access a game console hooked up to the Internet. To move, you had the stick and buttons on the controller. To talk you had a keyboard, and to see, you had a TV screen. That was it.

There was no electricity in Versus Town. No gas lines or water mains. People who lived in a digital world never grew thirsty. They never felt cold, they never cooked. No one had to turn on the lights in a world made of light. There wasn't a single convenience store, movie theater, or ballpark. At night, sometime between ten o'clock and five the next morning, I log in and Tetsuo comes to Versus Town. A make-believe man in a make-believe city. He was new there, and he had come for one thing: to fight.

Versus Town was an online fighting game that used the Internet to bring together players from around the world. They fought each other using their controllers to manipulate the characters on the screen. No two characters were alike. Their polygonal bodies moved with supernatural precision motion-captured by state-of-the-art technology from real martial artists. Polygonal warriors for a polygonal world.

The digital shops and houses, light poles and trash cans, glimmering cel-shaded and textured signs—all this meant nothing to the people who lived in Versus Town. They ran the streets in search of their next battle. Their arms were made to punch, their legs to kick. Even their heads were weapons; no thoughts flitted behind their lifeless eyes.

The capoeirista a fading memory, Tetsuo ran down Main Street toward the arena—a route he could have navigated blindfolded. That was where everyone would be.

Tetsuo pushed open a door of frosted glass and stepped into the arena. A poster advertising the upcoming second season tournament hung on the marble-textured wall. The tournament was scheduled to open the last week of June, less than a month away. Tetsuo would be entering, and he meant to win.

Tetsuo headed for a private training room at the edge of the arena where he proceeded to practice his combo moves on a wooden sparring dummy. His usual pre-fight warm-up. Countless characters were engaged in matches in the fighting rings at his back. There were fighters from every school imaginable: snake boxing, wrestling, drunken fist, and sumo, to name a few.

Two characters stood at the far right edge of my screen, not fighting, but chatting. Whoever they were, they knew their way around a keyboard; the text in the bubbles over their heads scrolled by in a blur. They were standing a good distance away, so the words appeared somewhat squished, but I could still make them out.

> Probably a snake boxer.

A gaudy T-shirt was textured across the man's chest. His stance labeled him a karateka like Tetsuo. The other character was a lightweight fighter, probably a jujutsuka. He wore a white sparring suit with a brown, pleated hakama skirt that hung from his waist. On his feet were a pair of straw sandals the color of fresh-cut grass.

> Probably?

The karateka's answer bubbled onto the screen.

> Nobody knows for sure.
> He really that good?
> They say he beat one of the top four.
> Who?
> 963.

The "top four" wasn't an official distinction in Versus Town, but it carried such weight that it may as well have been. As far as the players were concerned, the four best characters in the game were Pak, a snake boxer; Keith, a capoeirista; Tanaka, an eagle claw stylist; and 963, a jujutsuka. But it was Pak who outshone all the rest. He had won the first season tournament with barely a scratch. Beating Pak was the dream of every player in Versus Town.

I gave my hands a rest and turned my attention to their conversation.

> Can't you just ask him who it was?
> I did.
> And?
> He was alone over in Sanchōme when he got ganked. Never saw who it was.

The mysterious character stalking Sanchōme was a common topic these days.

> PK?
> Everyone's a PK in VT. It was just another street fight.
> Why doesn't he try for a rematch?
> This guy's way too good.
> He can't be all that.

> We're talking Lord British tough. No one's ever beat him.
> Maybe it was some kind of script?

People paid a monthly fee to play *Versus Town*, so the players were more than players, they were customers. Scripted events were one trick the game developers used to keep customers entertained and online. But the karateka was clearly unconvinced.

> Nah, I'm telling you, it wasn't a script.
> I'd like to see him for myself.
> He only fights the best. If you're not in the top ten, he won't give you the time of day.
> I don't buy it. They're losing players, so they wrote some script to stir up some talk is all.
> /shrug Maybe.
> One of the top four's a snake boxer, right?
> Yeah.
> Then it must be him.
> It's a different character.
> So maybe he's playing an alt. He's the same school.
> 963 said he played different.
> You can't tell from one fight. A fight he lost, by the way.
> True that.
> So why's he ganking people?
> Maybe he likes taking the piss out of players who think they're masters of the universe.
> Why all the secret ninja shit?
> That way if he loses, nobody knows it's him. He's not embarrassed on his main.
> Makes sense.
> Good enough for me.
> You're probably right.

I found myself staring blankly at the screen. A chime

sounded, warning me I'd been inactive, and I realized their conversation had ended.

Light spilled from the TV into my dimly lit room. The digital clock on my DVR read 11:45. The air had grown damp, and my hand was uncomfortably warm where my palm met the stick. The karateka and his jujutsuka friend had long since logged out.

I heard a *tap tap tap* on the roof, rhythmic and faint. Rain. Outside the street was quiet, the wail of the police siren a distant memory.

For some reason, I couldn't get the snake boxer from Sanchōme out of my head. Tonight's score: 42 wins, 0 losses, 3 ties.

IT WAS RAINING. There was more wet in the air than air, making it difficult to breathe. The water that had soaked through my shoes leeched warmth from the tips of my toes. There was a growing puddle, a shiny disc of reflected fluorescent light, beneath my umbrella where it leaned against the desk.

I sat in a small classroom, two seats from the dingy wall at the back of the room, staring up at the flickering fluorescent light overhead. The patter of raindrops against the windows. The squeak of chalk on the blackboard. Whispers that died before you could guess where they'd come from. It all formed a pastiche of sound FX over the music playing in my headphones.

My logic instructor, Professor Uemura, loved tracking attendance. It was a real fetish of his. He would hand out cards at the start of each class and collect them after the bell rang to dismiss us. If you brought the card with you, you could show up right before class ended to turn it in for full credit. The trick was having the right card; he used about twenty different kinds. So despite the fact it was the first period on a Monday morning, the classroom was full.

Most of the students sat hunched over their desks, dutifully transcribing the lecture notes from the blackboard to their notebooks. A handful of people were lower still on their desks, busy trying to make up for the sleep they'd lost getting to class. I was the only one in the room looking up at the ceiling. I stifled a yawn. Professor Uemura continued scribbling on the board. He could crank out a page's worth of notes every two minutes. The man had a real gift for writing on a blackboard. Some of his lectures came dangerously close to filling up twenty pages.

On the desk in front of me were a limp sheet of wide-ruled

loose-leaf paper and a blue attendance card. The paper was only a quarter full. Five minutes in I'd given up on the whole thing. The real mistake was embarking on such a noble endeavor in the first place. In the time it took me to write down one character, he'd written somewhere between three and five. For each line I copied down, he got another two lines ahead. When the eraser came sweeping down in a remorseless arc over the words I was still struggling to copy, I knew I was done with my mechanical pencil for the day. Since then I'd been lost in the world of portable music.

Had I known this professor would be such an attendance Nazi, I'd never have taken the class. My friends had lured me in with assurances of easy credits. Sure, all you had to do was show up. But showing up meant subjecting yourself to ninety minutes of paint-dryingly boring lectures.

I flicked my mechanical pencil with my index finger. It spun across the palm of my hand, slick with humidity and sweat, rotating about 45 degrees too far before it went tumbling across the loose-leaf paper to land on the desk with a hard clatter. The guy in the chair in front of me shifted slightly in his seat. The fluorescent lighting cast a pale green shadow on his shirt. I felt a faint breath of warm air caress my cheek under the weight of the stagnant air.

I hated rain. Elementary school had been a string of field trips played out against a backdrop of rainy days. Our athletic meets were regularly rained out and rescheduled from the weekends to Wednesdays. The first time I worked up the courage to tell a girl I liked her, an unseasonal typhoon was roaring outside. I later broke up with said girl during a driving rain that fell all day. On the day I learned I failed the college entrance exam, and a year later when I finally passed it, a drizzle so fine it fell like mist from a humidifier blanketed the city. I'd even heard from my mother that on the day I was born, a nasty day in late June right in the middle of the rainy season, the air had been a thick pea soup, damp and clinging.

So I was generally unpleasant on mornings during the rainy season. That I had previously acquired the particular variety of attendance card handed out today—and thus had shown up at the beginning of class for nothing—did nothing to lighten my mood.

"This seat taken?" It was a soft sound, barely enough to derail my train of thought. I looked up from the desk. "Your bag. It's taking up a seat." She took a deep breath, chest rising, falling. The gentle curve of her bangs brushed restlessly against her forehead. A steady stream of pinky nail–sized water drops dribbled from the tip of the umbrella clutched in her right hand.

I pulled the earbud from my left ear.

"Can I sit here?" she mouthed more than spoke. Her voice had the saccharine squeak of an anime character.

I glanced around the room. Pairs of long, rectangular desks stretched from just in front of the lectern to the back of the classroom. Each desk sat three people, and they were all full. All, that is, except the seat next to mine.

I moved my bag out of the seat. The girl gave a quick nod of thanks and sat down. I restored my headphone to its place in my left ear, and the music blossomed from tinny monaural to full and vibrant stereo. Resting my chin on my hands, I resumed my observation of the fluorescent lights.

Fluorescent lights flicker off and on at a rate of something like fifty or sixty times per second. I read somewhere that there's a tiny little man who runs electricity through the mercury vapor inside the tube to make it glow. When the light flickers, it's the little man catching his breath. And when the light gets old and starts randomly blinking off and on, well, that's the little man's fault too. Sometimes I wonder if it would be possible to see each individual cycle of light—on off, on off—the way swordsmen in samurai novels can peer through each individual drop of rain as it falls from the eaves of a roof. There are people who can push a button sixteen times per second, so why not?

I shifted my gaze from the light to the girl sitting beside me. She was still getting her things out of her bag. Her notebook was easily three times as thick as mine, and her mechanical pencil wasn't 0.5 mm—the accepted standard—but a hefty 0.7. Clearly, she didn't mess around.

She opened her notebook. Neat rows of kanji filled the college-ruled pages from the top-left corner to the bottom-right. Her handwriting could have passed for the work of a professional calligrapher. It was about two hundred fifty-six times neater than mine. If you measured the space between characters with calipers, they'd probably have no more than a millimeter's variation. She had probably sent off for one of those calligraphy-writing kits they advertise at the back of manga. And it hadn't just sat around on a shelf collecting dust once it arrived. No, this was a girl that did her homework.

She scowled and let out a long frustrated sigh. Reaching once more into her bag she pulled out a plastic case. Within rested a pair of round, silver-rimmed glasses with extremely small lenses. She placed the glasses on her face with both hands and promptly joined the masses copying notes off the board.

She was left-handed. Her right hand smoothed back her jet-black hair while her left produced picture-perfect characters with breathtaking speed. The silver rims of her glasses scattered metallic light as she looked at the blackboard. Still wet from the rain, the shoulders of her Naples yellow blouse clung to her skin. Her damp hair clumped together, casting a spiky anime-shadow across the back of her neck.

She had a faint, sweet scent about her, like the olive tree growing in our neighbor's yard. I felt my breath catch in my throat.

This wasn't the sort of girl who stockpiled attendance cards so she could sleep in. She highlighted passages in her textbook and notes, which strongly suggested she actually read them. She didn't cram for a test the night before, and she sure as hell never had to do a makeup test. She'd probably graduated with honors from a private high school. Daddy's little girl. Daddy the famously rich banker or politician. In short, she was just the kind of girl I wanted nothing to do with.

Making no effort to be quiet, I opened my bag and shoved my blank loose-leaf paper and mechanical pencil inside. I hefted the bag to my shoulder, pushed back from the desk, and stood.

"Mind handing this in for me?" I held out two blue attendance cards. Across one was scrawled Etsuro Sakagami, but the other was blank. It was the only spare blue card I had, but I didn't really care.

Her eyes opened wide behind those tiny glasses. "Today's blue," she muttered.

"What?"

"Today's cards. They're blue."

"Yeah, so?"

"The cat's blue. The one in Shinjuku. If you find it," she said with a smile, "all your dreams will come true." It was an unlikely smile. The sort of smile you'd expect from someone who'd just returned from a grueling ten-year journey and stumbled upon the blue cat of happiness. If you sold that smile in a hamburger shop, it'd sell better than the fries. That was what it looked like to me, anyway.

I stood there holding my bag as Professor Uemura pounded at the blackboard with a nublet of chalk not long for this world. I had about twenty seconds before he turned around to face the class. I was fairly certain the blue animal from the urban legend to which she was referring was a bird, not a cat, but instead of pointing out her mistake, I forced a smile. "Whatever you say. Thanks."

"Um, your notes." A quarter-filled sheet of paper still lay there on the desk. The fluorescent lights turned it the same shade of sickly green as that guy's shirt.

"Toss 'em. I don't need 'em."

I turned away before she could speak and made my escape.

I hadn't given her the card to be nice, and I wasn't flirting. It just didn't seem fair that I should get credit for attending because I had learned to game the system, while this girl who went to class and actually paid attention would be counted absent. *It was that sigh of hers*, I thought. It planted the seeds of guilt in me. Giving her one of my cards was the only way I had of paying penance.

Almost-empty bag and soggy umbrella in hand, I opened the door that led out into the hallway. I pushed a button on my music player to skip to the next track—I needed something more upbeat. Rain drummed against the windows rhythmically, like water from a sprinkler, as the chill of the air folded itself around me.

~

I walked along Ome Highway toward Shinjuku. It was 8:57, that strange time when the Shinjuku of the night prepared for sleep, and the Shinjuku of the day crawled out from under its collective futon. The only people wandering the streets at this hour were university students, the homeless, and people on their way home from jobs in the sex trade.

When it wasn't raining, I was actually fond of tramping around Shinjuku without any particular destination. If I'd had someplace to go, I would have gone there, but RL—real life—was vast and confusing, and I couldn't figure out where I should be. In this city, there weren't any NPCs standing around to hint at where the next big event would be, no online guides to point you in the right direction. Since I had nothing better to do, I resolved to walk around until I wore myself out and I couldn't lift my legs another step. There wouldn't be any battles, no objectives reached or quests completed, but the exhaustion would make me feel as though I'd done something with my day. Or just maybe, if I walked off every last bit of the grid that made up this RL city, I'd stumble across something special.

A dream world reflected in tiny drops of rain surrounded me. A low mist hung in the sky, obscuring the skyscrapers and the looming hulk of Tokyo City Hall from view. The only thing that seemed real in the haze was a sports car parked illegally with one wheel on the sidewalk. The car was blood red. I quickened my pace and vaulted across a puddle of water.

My university was in west Shinjuku. I turned right along Ome Highway in front of the Shinjuku Police Station and continued walking south past Keio Plaza Hotel. I turned again just after the Shinjuku Monolith Building, and from there it was a straight shot to the trains. The scenery in west Shinjuku could get a little monotonous. There were plenty of freaks hanging around to spice things up, but the real show was out at the east side of the station.

I came out of the underpass as a Yamanote Line train raced by, and metallic sound FX reverberated ninety centimeters above my head. I crossed beneath the large Alta screen and headed for Kabuki-chō. I still didn't know where I was going. Wherever my feet took me, I guess. If you made it through the squalor of Kabuki-chō Itchōme and kept on going, you'd come out in Nichōme, the gay district.

I found her on the outskirts of Kabuki-chō, standing by a place that was either up-and-coming or down-and-out—it was hard to tell. The surrounding buildings took the word seedy to entirely new levels. Spots of rust marred the iron fire escapes, and everywhere were stacks of crates brimming with empty beer bottles. The stench of stale, drunken vomit permeated the air in front of the bar, or pub, or whatever this establishment was supposed to be. A blue laser traced the name of the place on the asphalt in front of the door. In daylight, it was impossible to make out what it said. The oscillator in the laser must have been broken, because every few seconds the image would wobble and the beam of blue light would shoot off in some random direction.

I'd seen the woman before on other walks through Shinjuku

about this time of day and had pegged her for a prostitute, but it was just a guess. I didn't know the first thing about her. Whoever she was, she couldn't have been the most model citizen if a class-cutting, street-wandering student had run into her enough times to know her by sight.

She didn't look especially young or old, and it was hard to tell if she was wearing any makeup. Her hair had been dyed a reddish brown, and she wore it long and disheveled. Her clothing looked expensive, but she hadn't gone out for any frills. Across her shoulders she wore a shawl, or maybe it was cloak, but she always had it.

I don't know how long she'd been a fixture here. The files in my head for this city only went back as far as April. Maybe it had only been a few months like me, or maybe she'd lived here a decade. We'd made eye contact plenty of times but never exchanged any words, so I didn't have much to go on.

Whenever I came across her, she'd be standing there staring off at nothing in particular, with the look of a bat just waking from hibernation, searching for its first meal in months. I don't even know if bats hibernate. In the narrow strip of sky before her eyes, a ragged clothesline flapped in the wind, oscillating at a rate of roughly sixteen times per second.

I chose that day to talk to her because I got it in my head that maybe this woman, standing under that blue laser in an obscure corner of the most cliché slum in Shinjuku, might know something about the cat. True, the only thing in common between the two was the color blue, but I had a feeling that the cat was the only flag waiting to be triggered to start the next event in my life.

"Have you seen it?"

At the sound of my voice, the bat lady shifted her eyes. It was the only indication she'd heard me at all; her face and body remained carved from stone.

"Seen what?" She had a deep voice.

"A cat, actually."

"Calico? Black? White with black spots? What's the tail look like?"

"Nah, it's not like that. It's a blue cat."

The woman moved. She let out a tired sigh, the sigh of a middle-aged man who knows his best years are behind him, and placed her hand on her hip. I hadn't noticed it while she was standing there, but she had all the right curves in all the right places. "You too, huh?"

"Excuse me?" As I spoke, the bat lady started walking toward me. The wayward laser display cut across her leg, painting some undecipherable glyph on the white flesh of her calf. "You mean other people are looking for it?"

"It's an urban legend. All the girls around here have heard of it. You know those dyed chicks they sell at fairs? They say some pet store owner got the idea to do the same thing with cats, but one of them, a kitten, died. Now it haunts the streets of the city."

"It's a ghost?"

"That's the story." The girl in class had said that finding the cat would make dreams come true, but the ghost of a dead puss out for vengeance seemed more the stuff of nightmares than dreams. The bat lady pulled a long, slender cigarette out from under her cloak and lit it. "You won't have much luck during the day. Better try at night."

"Ah, right. Ghosts don't like the daylight and all that."

"Won't be easy finding it. I hope you do, though."

"Nah, I'm not really lookin'."

"Oh? Don't give up before you even start. Who knows? Maybe you'll find something, maybe you won't. It's the searching that counts. Good luck." She turned suddenly in a flutter of hair and fabric and walked inside. I knew she was a bat.

I didn't go back to school that afternoon.

~

The next morning I missed the train I normally took to get to class. I ride the Tōbu Tōjō line from Mizuhodai Station to Ikebukuro, where I switch to the southbound Yamanote line. It was a little after rush hour, so the trains weren't too crowded.

The metal-on-metal sound FX of wheels on rails pierced through the soundtrack pumping in my headphones. A dim urban landscape scrolled past outside the windows. It wasn't raining, but the sky was clad in gray. I leaned back against the vertical handrail beside the door, taking in from the corner of my eye the brightly colored posters hanging in the aisle. For about one stop the rail had felt cool and refreshing, but it had already warmed to match my body temperature.

By June, the crowds had usually thinned out. Every April, the trains overflowed with overeager freshmen, but a month or two of school was enough to dull anyone's enthusiasm. I hated each and every one of them. They were scrubs, ignorant of the laws of the rails. The subtle, silent language of the rush-hour commuter was foreign to them, so they shouted like tourists trying to make themselves understood. They bitched. They moaned. They caused trouble. They turned molehills into mountains. They were a pain in the ass.

I was a veteran. I'd been battle-hardened thanks to four years in rush hours—three in high school, one before entering university. I could spot a scrub a mile away. The hicks fresh off the farm were the worst. I'd even seen them in all-out brawls with salarymen, and ninety-nine times out of a hundred it was the poor salaryman who'd been wronged in the first place.

The trains were the domain of the salarymen. On the streets you cut dump trucks, taxis, and pizza delivery boys on their 50 cc bikes extra slack. You looked the other way if they bent the rules because you were just a guest on their turf. On trains it was the salarymen. They were holy men and this was their sacred ground. So no matter how empty the car was, I was content to stand quietly in my little corner by the door, out of respect.

My train pulled in to Shinjuku Station.

I set off on foot down Ome Highway. Before noon, campus was even emptier than the trains on the Yamanote. I glanced at the bulletin board on my way in and headed for my sociology class. The lecture had started seventy-five minutes ago; my timing couldn't have been better. I took a seat along the window side of the lecture hall, two rows from the back, and filled in my name on the attendance sheet lying on the desk.

A man with thinning hair stood in front of the blackboard, lecturing with a mic in one hand. His hair looked like strips of dried seaweed. The color, the thickness, the sheen—perfect verisimilitude. The professor's name was...I forget.

I cut the volume on my music, and the lecture came seeping into my ears. Seaweed Head was explaining that many animals live in groups as a way of self-regulating the population of the species.

There's a type of wheat-eating beetle that takes up cannibalism when the swarm grows too dense. Rats raised in overcrowded conditions show signs of mental disorders. A species of rabbit living in the U.S. state of Minnesota develops liver failure and dies when the population density of the warren rises too high. Seaweed Head claimed that before the spread of democracy, humans had instinctively limited their own population. The advancement of civilization was undermining a basic societal function. It didn't sound like the sort of ideas a sociology professor should be espousing.

Uncomfortably warm air filled the lecture hall from floor to ceiling. I felt an ache deep inside, at the core of my being. I stared at the attendance sheet and looked around the room. There were no familiar faces, no familiar names.

Most of the few friends I had made were gone by the end of May. They weren't strutting around Shinjuku confident of their intellectual superiority or copping an attitude on the trains. They'd just faded away. I played online games with one of them, but lately I hadn't seen him there or in RL. In a sociological sense, he had been a member of the university student species living on an overcrowded campus and had died for the good of the group. Maybe I would be next. If the natural order held sway on university grounds, it seemed inevitable.

Too stubborn to know when I was beat, I pored over the attendance sheet again and again. One name appeared more often than any other in the top row. My circle of friends had settled onto the bottom of the roster, and *she* had found a comfortable perch at the top. If I could write in her two-hundred-fifty-six-times-neater-than-mine handwriting, maybe scratching out notes during class wouldn't be so bad. But if there was a proportional relationship between time spent studying and handwriting legibility, I was more than happy to rough it out with my hen scratches.

More sound FX signaled the end of class. Clutching the attendance sheet, I walked down to the front of the room and placed it on the podium. I turned to head back up the steps and there she was, sitting in the front row. The same face I'd seen from a mere eighty centimeters' distance the day before.

She was wearing a collared silver-gray shirt with buttons down the front. Her 0.7 mm mechanical pencil rested in her hand. The strands of her neatly trimmed shoulder-length hair seemed less coarse than they had yesterday. Her glasses were nowhere to be seen.

I walked past without a word. She noticed me and looked up. I saw her lips form the word *thanks*. Her lips kept moving, but I couldn't make out the rest of the sentence. I pulled the headphone out of my left ear and looked down at her. Today I was going to make an effort to communicate.

"Hey."

"Thanks for yesterday," she said with an awkward smile.

I told her it was no big deal and then hurried up the steps, once again turning away before she could speak. Fragments of a dozen things I might have said to her flashed through my head. *It wouldn't have been fair. I was just covering my own ass.*

We're two very different kinds of people. But none of it would have done any good. I decided to skip my afternoon class and went straight home instead.

I PRESSED THE 🅰️ BUTTON. With a *click*, I became Tetsuo.

The same turquoise blue sky greeted me. The same light poles throwing their slightly jagged shadows on the ground. Beyond the lights stood the entrance to the town, barren and empty. Tetsuo winked into existence at that entrance, the same way he always did.

Versus Town was an MMO—a massively multiplayer online fighting game. That means you didn't fight against a computer opponent; you played the game against other players, all connected through the same network.

At any given moment, dozens of characters might appear and disappear at any of the city's twenty-four gates. Passing through a gate in the first district, Itchōme, would save your character's win/loss data. Itchōme was also the place to go if you wanted to change your character's appearance, fighting school, or weight class. There was even a message board set up offering players yet another way to communicate with each other. In practice, people rarely altered their character's appearance, school, or weight class, and if you were already online you didn't need any more ways to communicate, so none of those features saw much use. Itchōme was huge, and the first thing everyone did when they got there was speed-dash out of it as fast as they could. Tetsuo found the right side of Main Street and started running.

There was no way to tell the identity of the player behind a character. It might be some salaryman you'd never met in your life or it could be the guy you sat next to in class who lived across the street. It could be anyone. The only thing that showed up on the screen was the character the player had created. It wasn't much, but when you stepped up to go head to head with someone, it was everything.

When you got right down to it, a fighting game was nothing more than an elaborate match of rock-paper-scissors in which you were allowed to cheat. If you thought you saw rock coming, you gave the sign for paper. If it looked like scissors, you responded with rock. When someone threw a punch at you, you blocked. Punches and kicks don't hurt while you're blocking, so your attacker would probably try for a throw next. You couldn't block a throw, but every throw could be countered with the right throw break. Throw breaks, in turn, left you vulnerable to strikes.

You had to read the battle, wait for your opponent to expose a weakness. Fake with rock, move in with scissors. Land blows where you could. Keep unavoidable damage to a bare minimum. That was what a virtual character like Tetsuo had to do to survive in this virtual town.

Tetsuo pushed the frosted glass door open and stepped into the arena. The arena was located in the second district of Versus Town, Nichōme. Log in and out in Itchōme, fight in Nichōme: Tetsuo's daily commute.

The third and final district was Sanchōme, but it didn't have anything to do with the meat of the game. After I first opened my account, I'd taken Tetsuo for a spin around Sanchōme, but it wasn't much more than a polygonal slum.

When they could hook your brain up to electrodes like in those old sci-fi novels and movies so you could feel, smell, even taste the virtual world around you, a place like Sanchōme might not be so bad. But the residents of Versus Town couldn't touch, they couldn't smell, and they couldn't taste. They could only fight. The only windows players had into Versus Town were their lousy monitors. The only way to control your character was with one stick and three buttons.

Tetsuo walked across the arena to the training rooms in back for his usual combo warm-up routine. A gamer that relied on fast reflexes was a lot like a katana. To stay sharp, you had to hone your skills each and every day. If you took a day off, you were that much weaker.

For the most part, action games required your muscles to learn certain patterns of motion and execute them with blinding speed at precisely the right moment. Get carried away, and it could have a negative impact on you in RL. Suppose you spent ten hours a day playing *Tetris*. Next thing you know you're walking down the street thinking about where to place that nice square building up ahead.

Fighting games are the same. Everyone sacrifices something from RL to spend time fighting in Versus Town.

Tanaka was in the arena with dozens of characters in the queue, waiting their turn to fight him. He was one of the top four, the best in Versus Town. Everyone knew who they were, so when one of them showed up in the arena, an endless stream of characters would arrive to sign up for a match. Tonight was no exception.

Since the time I opened my *Versus Town* account, I had wanted to see Tetsuo join the top four. All I had to do was defeat Pak, the best of the best, and Tetsuo would reign supreme. I didn't doubt for a second that everyone else waiting in that arena queue had the same idea.

I wasn't after virtual fame or notoriety. Tetsuo was already well into the ranks of the elite, and he never had trouble finding someone willing to face him in the arena. But if I made it into the top four, the internal barometer I had of my own skill would finally be calibrated against something like an objective set of standards.

Games are just another form of entertainment. Being good at a game doesn't raise your grades, and it doesn't help you find a job. It wouldn't do much of anything to help you in RL. Maybe that's why I wanted some sign, some token of achievement in the virtual world to show for my hard work.

Tetsuo finished practicing on the training dummy. He stepped out onto the arena floor. There were thirty-three people in Tanaka's queue. I wanted to put Tetsuo up against him, but I wasn't in the mood to wait half the night to do it.

Tanaka was fighting a snake boxer in the middle of the arena. It looked like a good match. The snake boxer was a newcomer, someone I'd never seen before. Newcomer or no, he was holding his own against Tanaka. Come to think of it, the character that ganked 963 out in Sanchōme was supposed to be a snake boxer too. *Hmm.*

The match ended. The snake boxer had won. Text bubbles started popping up over the heads of the characters crowded near Tetsuo.

> Some guy just beat Tanaka!
> No way.
> Screen shot or it didn't happen.

As others read the bubbles and pecked out answers in reply, a chain reaction threatened to fill the screen with text.

> Who did it?
> I dunno.
> What's the big deal? Even Tanaka has to lose sometime.
> Dude, a scrub doesn't just come along and wtfpwn Tanaka.
> You think it was that guy from Sanchōme?
> We just witnessed history, man. History!
> Damn, I need some food.
> I go bio for a bath, and all hell breaks loose!
> I can't see. Is this even hitting you?
> TEXT BUBBLES ARE ANNOYING.
> Dude, caps.

The comments rose one after another. It was like watching

a cel-shaded pot of boiling water spill across the arena as the giddy wave of hysteria spread.

Tanaka might play a hundred matches a day, so on average he was bound to lose two or three. Anyone could get tired and have an off night. It was the second season tournament that had everyone buzzing about the loss. It was getting closer, and you could feel the tension mounting.

Everyone gathered in the arena was there to put the polish on their game. *If one of the top four can lose, maybe I have a shot.* The place was a tinderbox, and that one upset was the spark. Of course most of the people there were like kids standing on the school roof watching a typhoon roll in. When the storm came, they were going to be blown away. There were only sixteen slots in the finals.

Tanaka would make the cut. Maybe the snake boxer who just beat him would make it too. And Tetsuo sure as hell planned to make it.

The cumulonimbus of text bubbles covering half the screen cleared, leaving Tanaka standing at the center. A bubble appeared above his head.

> How 'bout another match?
> Sorry, getting sleepy. Maybe next time.

I glanced at the readout on my DVR. 11:10. *Versus Town* was just getting started at 11:10. It had to be an excuse. No way this guy was sleepy. While I considered his bald-faced lie, he actually logged out, right then and there. Tanaka started a match with the next character in the queue.

Something dawned on me later that night as I was fighting. That snake boxer was probably just some kid in elementary school.

~

Time is a limited resource, one for which online games have a voracious appetite. The more of this resource you spent in the virtual world, the less you had left over for the real one. The opposite was true too. Spend too much time in RL, and you wouldn't have enough left over to do the things you wanted to do online. *Versus Town* may not have been as bad as those role-playing games that made you trade countless hours of your life to level up your character, but it birthed its fair share of sun-fearing basement-dwellers all the same.

Back when I had just entered university, before I'd ever been to Versus Town or created Tetsuo, I had one friend in RL I used to talk online gaming with. He was from up north, Hokkaido, and had come all the way down to Tokyo for school. He lived alone.

One day I noticed that he had started wearing his hair in a ponytail. That was the first sign of trouble. When I asked him about it, he said he'd been too busy to go out and have it cut. Pretty soon he stopped going to class. Whenever I was on my PC, he'd message me how bored he was, that he had nothing to do. I told him that if he was so bored, he should try going to class. Apparently he wasn't *that* bored.

We had met and become friends through gaming. He poured almost all the resources he had into the virtual world. Maybe it was because he'd lost interest in the real one. There was a gleam in his eye when he talked about online gaming that was absent when we talked about anything else. Gaming was the one topic he could carry on a conversation about, which worked when it was just him and me, but as soon as you added a third person to the equation things started to fall apart. Little by little, he dropped out of our circle of friends.

I stopped by his place once around the end of April to check on him. He lived in a studio apartment that shared a communal toilet. There wasn't a shower at all. The storm shutters covering the window drooped on their hinges, permitting a narrow shaft of concentrated sunlight into the room. Limned in cream-yellow light, the minute hand of the clock hanging on the wall ticked away the hours. Every time a truck drove by, his bookshelf would shudder, and the glass doors would creak loudly.

My friend's skin was pale and hung loosely on his thin frame. It looked as though he had gone weeks without seeing the sun. Or a bath. I was still paying him occasional visits then, so he hadn't entirely given up on shaving yet. A centimeter of stubble bristled on the bottom of his chin. The question *How long does it take to grow a centimeter of facial hair?* flashed through my mind.

I can still hear him telling me how tired he was of RL. He said it was more trouble than it was worth, and I think he really believed it. Pretty soon he stopped leaving his apartment altogether.

I knew he was slipping off the deep end, but there was nothing I could do to stop him. Or maybe there was, and I just couldn't figure out what it was. Now I'd never know. The only thing I could do was talk to him, try not to make things worse. In the end, it wasn't enough.

Maybe a real friend would have been able to stop him from succumbing to his addiction. He had thrown away his chance at university and now spent his days sitting in a darkened room, staring into a monitor. He did all his shopping at convenience stores in the middle of the night. Most of his conversations took place in chat windows. He hardly ever spoke. Anyone on the outside looking in would have thought he was miserable.

All for a game. Any sane person wouldn't be able to comprehend it. Count yourself lucky if you don't.

Online games are only good for *otaku* and the chronically unemployed. If you don't fall into either of those two categories, keep walking the straight and narrow. Nothing to see here. The less you know about online games, the better. You can live your life, fall in love, grow old, and no one will point and laugh at you for never having played an online game. That's a promise.

Games in general are a waste of time, but online games are the worst. Mark my words. Still, I find myself wondering sometimes, if playing games is such a waste of time, what makes time spent in RL so inherently worthwhile? Hanging out with friends, laughing, fighting, studying your ass off for tests—these everyday experiences, a lot of which could only be called boring, form the foundation on which our lives are built, but I don't think you can say, categorically, that they're any more valuable than experiences in a virtual world.

My generation was raised on video games. We were the first to grow up playing them. We traded our pink left thumbs for hardened calluses by pushing too hard on control pads. We sat awake in bed dreaming up ways to take down the next boss. There were moments of clarity, sure. Sometimes the thought that it was all a colossal waste of time even crossed our minds. But it didn't stop us from playing.

In theory, it was possible to earn a living online by participating in RMT. That's Real Money Trading. A quick search of any auction site would turn up countless listings for people offering virtual money in exchange for the real deal. Rare items sometimes sold for astronomical amounts. Buyers were people with money in RL but without the time to play the game for themselves. Sellers were people with nothing but time on their hands, and no RL money. By parceling up and selling off time spent playing the game, you could earn the money you needed to live.

In other words, it was a job. In that, it was really no different than what millions of so-called blue collar workers did each and every day. There were those who claimed anything virtual was worthless, but they were wrong. In the right hands, nothing could be transformed into something. It was like the service industry. There was no substance to it, but that didn't mean there wasn't profit to be had. It was something we all understood.

But my friend and I never did anything like that. People with the brains to pull off that sort of operation didn't get addicted to online games in the first place. The kind of person who could look at a virtual world as just another communication tool and put that information to use in RL would never organize their lives around playing some game.

Why? Because the instant you started dealing with RMT, the virtual and the real became bound together with numbers and symbols. Once that happened, you couldn't help but realize that the virtual world wasn't fun at all. In fact, it was just as boring and ordinary as RL, and just as worthless. You were running those childhood dreams through an RL calculator and spitting out their worth, if any, and the present value of the future cash flows they could be expected to generate.

So we avoided that scene. We didn't harden the skin on our thumbs to fine Corinthian leather in hopes of cashing in. We played games to play games.

I didn't have the words to stop my friend from traveling down the road he'd chosen. It reminded me of the end of *The Lord of the Rings*, when the elves sailed off into the True West. I was a hobbit who knew the power of the ring only too well, but I was Merry to his Frodo. He knew that where he was going there was no coming back, and a part of me was a little jealous of that determination. I felt the power of the ring, even felt my hold on RL slipping away at times, but I hesitated. I lacked the courage to take that final step, even while deep inside, I hoped to make that journey myself someday.

My friend managed to eke out a living on his allowance for a little while, but eventually he had to go back to Hokkaido. His cell number and email worked through the end of May, but by June even those had been disconnected. In the end it wasn't the west he disappeared into, but the north.

Sooner or later, everybody dies. I figure it's best to spend your life doing what you enjoy. Every morning when I stand and look into the mirror, that time is still my own. I wonder how much longer that will last.

These are the sorts of things that run through my head each night while Tetsuo fights in the arena.

The clock on my DVR read 6:15. Morning had stolen up on me. I could hear birds chirping through my shutters. My room was much warmer than it should have been for June thanks to the residual heat from the television and game console's having been on all night. Locked in the same position for hours, my knees creaked in protest as I stretched my legs.

Tanaka had logged out hours ago. The identity of the snake boxer who'd beaten him was still gnawing at me, but I didn't have a clue whether or not he was the same character who'd been ganking people down in Sanchōme. Tanaka's only defeat for the night had been at the hands of the mystery snake boxer.

The night's score for Tetsuo: 97 wins, 2 losses.

FEEBLE SUNLIGHT BATHED MY DESK. The air was still. Outside the window, row upon row of feathery clouds drifted through the Shinjuku sky. It was almost summer, but even in a long-sleeve shirt I could still feel the chill in the air. I was sitting by the window in a seat two rows from the back of a small, dimly lit classroom, listening to my economics professor.

The room was alive with sound FX. Gusts of wind rattling the window panes. Pencil lead gliding across paper. The guy in front of me rocking in his seat.

It was 11:28 AM. I ventured a quick stretch. I'd just crossed the halfway mark of my second ninety-minute lecture of the day, and my health gauge was running low. It was all I could do to grip my mechanical pencil in my right hand. The disks of my back were screaming in agony. Expecting students to sit for ninety minutes at a time in such poorly designed chairs raised serious questions about the Japanese educational system. The chairs department stores lined up beside the stairs so elderly shoppers could take a load off were the pinnacle of comfort by comparison. I was starting to consider myself a man of preternatural endurance, a human copy machine whose sole purpose on this earth was to transcribe text from the blackboard onto sheets of loose-leaf paper for hours on end.

The professor, a man of about fifty, was delivering an impassioned speech in front of the blackboard. Mr. Yamawhatsit or Mr. Somethingawa. I couldn't remember his name. I rested my chin on folded hands, only half listening to the lecture.

If you had two identical widgets, and the price of one of them dropped, the cheaper widget would sell more units. The drop in price would translate into an effective increase in real wages. If, however, the cheap widget was of inferior quality and the standard of living rose, he claimed, people would stop buying the cheap widget.

RL was full of convoluted laws in which I had little to no interest. Thankfully, the topic of the next lecture would be Game Theory. I didn't know what games had to do with economics, but it sounded like it might be something worth listening to.

Fifteen minutes before the end of class, the professor dropped a bombshell. "We finished early today, so I think we have time for a quiz." Ignoring the boos erupting from the seats, he started handing out the quiz. The stacks of neatly Xeroxed quiz papers gave the lie to his "finishing early." Clearly this was a setup, but I held my tongue and filled in my name.

The sunlight shining into the room traced the shadow of the windowsill on the dingy recycled paper. I attempted to read a few of the questions but soon gave up. They may as well have been written in Greek. It was an open-note quiz, but the only notes I had with me were from today, and this was only the second lecture I'd attended since the beginning of April.

Luckily, I knew that for quizzes like these, it was usually more important to be there to write your name on the paper than to actually answer the questions. It was actually a weird sort of luck that he had decided to give a quiz on one of the few days I'd shown up.

The professor told us we could leave once we'd finished. I hadn't written a thing other than my name, but I lacked the guts to walk up to the podium and hand in a blank sheet of paper. So I turned to my old pastime of staring up at the fluorescent lights.

Seven minutes before the end of class, a girl in the front row stood up. She'd been sitting smack dab in the middle of the row. She set her quiz on the podium and left without breaking her stride. The sort of people who voluntarily sat front and center were usually the ones who looked over their answers again and again before turning them in, even when they knew they were perfect. Guess you never can tell.

I watched the girl as she walked toward the door. She had on a moss-green jacket and a pair of soft-looking denim jeans. The bag slung over her shoulder was about three times the size of mine. Her neatly trimmed, shoulder-length hair bounced as she walked, alternately revealing and concealing the white nape of her neck. She wasn't wearing her glasses today.

As she walked past my desk, she dropped a notebook into the empty chair beside me. A name was written across the front. Fumiko something or other. An obvious reading for the kanji didn't come to mind.

Page after college-ruled page of letter perfect calligraphic text flashed before my eyes as I flipped through the notebook. Next to my sad loose-leaf sheets, Fumiko's notes looked as though they'd been shot out of a laser printer.

Why would she leave me her notes? What was in it for her? What was the catch? A dozen questions raced through my head, but I set them aside and got down to the business of copying answers from the page Fumiko had dog-eared.

More sound FX heralded the end of class. I turned in my quiz and left the room.

Fumiko stood in a patch of shade beside the door, resting her back against the rose-gray wall. I walked over to her.

"Thanks for the notes."

"Sure thing." That anime-saccharine voice. "Etsuro, right?"

"That's me."

"You only come to the classes they take attendance in."

"Looks like."

"I'm Fumiko Nagihara. A lot of people have trouble with the last name."

"Oh yeah?"

"It's kind of an unusual reading for those kanji, don't you think?"

"I guess."

"Right...So, you just showed up for the quiz today?"

"Not really. It was just a coincidence."

"Just a coincidence you happened to be here the one day we have a quiz?"

"That's right."

"That's quite a superpower you got there." Fumiko smiled her hamburger-shop smile.

I gave a noncommittal grunt, which she took as a cue to further mock my less-than-stellar attendance record. At least she went to the trouble of leavening her rude comments with another smile.

It turned out Fumiko and I had the same major. She claimed to have been there at orientation and the freshman party, but I couldn't recall seeing her. Then again, I was pretty bad when it came to remembering faces. In my best virtual scorekeeping mode, I told her this made us even at one win apiece. Fumiko headed off for her next class.

~

A hazy moon hung in the narrow sky over Shinjuku. Beneath, neon lights bathed the streets in garish reds, blues, and greens. My cheeks were flushed with heat, and the warm wind blowing out of the south wasn't helping.

It was 7:57 in the evening in Kabuki-chō Itchōme. The streets were aglow in synthetic light. After the lecture, some people from my class had invited me out, and we'd made a beeline for the bars.

By June, everyone had more or less sorted out who they were going to be friends with, and who they weren't. The people I would have called my friends were ghosts who attended the university in name and name alone. Just because people joined the same department when they started university didn't mean they had assigned seats next to each other like in junior high, and it was no guarantee they'd even end up taking the same classes. We all just happened to have more or less the same academic aptitude, and we'd all applied to and been accepted by the same university. So I might have known my classmates, but that didn't necessarily make them my friends. The brutal truth of it was that they had about as much to do with me as the bat lady, fresh out of hibernation, that I'd met on the streets of Shinjuku.

I didn't ordinarily join my classmates for drinks, and they didn't ordinarily invite me. I decided to go out with them on a whim. Spending time in the virtual world had stirred up memories of my friend who disappeared into the north, and I'd been feeling a little down that day. Maybe like attracts like, because we were all ready for a drink.

Later, when we left the bar, I broke off from a small group who decided they hadn't had enough to drink yet and started walking to the station.

Shinjuku overflowed with sound FX. Squadrons of feet pressing against asphalt. The hum of electricity through neon tubes. Laughs and shouts and the labored enthusiasm of street vendors hawking their wares blended together in a perfect harmony.

It was at the heart of this maelstrom of sound that I ran into Fumiko Nagihara. She was standing in front of an arcade near the Shinjuku Koma Theater. That a straitlaced girl like Fumiko wouldn't go out drinking with her classmates came as no surprise. That she would be out wandering around Kabuki-chō after the drinking had ended did. Good little girls were supposed to be at home at this hour, discussing the nightly news with their parents.

Fumiko's attention was riveted on the contents of a transparent bin at the entrance of the arcade. She wore the determined expression of a young child who thought she could bore a hole through the glass if only she stared hard enough.

Without warning, her burning gaze shifted to me. I can't say why, but in that instant I knew what it felt like to be a superhero with the weight of a weary world on his shoulders.

What self-respecting superhero could look into the face of a helpless girl, eyes brimming with hope, and not heed the call of justice?

"Etsuro."

"Hey."

"It's just too cute. I've *gotta* have it." She lifted her arm slowly, as though parting the air took great effort. Her outstretched finger came to rest pointing at a crane game. A menagerie of pink stuffed animals breathing fluffy golden flames peered out from within.

"I wouldn't waste my time," I said. "That claw looks loose."

"What, are you some kind of crane game expert?"

"If playing twice, maybe three times in my life makes me an expert, then yes."

"I'll just have to win it myself, then."

The soundtrack of the arcade was an old hit exhumed from the graveyard of folk songs past. Fumiko stepped up to the crane game. I could see the back of her neck, pale beneath the loose strands of her short bob haircut.

The claw missed the spot Fumiko was aiming for by about ten centimeters. She was five hundred yen poorer, and the plush object of her adoration hadn't even budged. It occurred to me that she might have some sort of congenital defect preventing her from understanding how these games worked. Say you've found the stuffed animal of your dreams, but it's buried under half a dozen other stuffed animals. Only a mental defective would go straight for the stuffed animal at the bottom. If you have a stack of dishes in the sink, you don't grab a dish out of the bottom of the stack. Where does this common sense go the minute people step up to a crane game? It works just like the dishes: you start with the one that's easiest to lift and work your way down.

When I explained this to Fumiko, she puffed out her cheeks in frustration. "So you're pretty good at games, huh?"

"Yeah, pretty good."

"Like, professional good?"

"I don't know any professional gamers."

"But you are good."

"Sure, I guess."

"Then you do it."

I arched my eyebrows. "I play shooters and fighting games. They're nothing like this. I hardly ever even *come* to arcades."

"Why not?"

"The games I play you play from home, over the Internet."

Fumiko was still puffing out her cheeks. On the face of it, we might have been tied at one win apiece, but if you weighed one pilfered attendance card against a notebook full of quiz answers, the attendance card came up awfully light.

I stepped in and put my hands on the controls.

On my first five hundred-yen coin, I won three stuffed animals. I even won the little flame-breathing guy, but Fumiko was unimpressed. She yanked on the strap of my bag and told me she wanted to try a different game. I told her it was a waste of time and money, but my objections were overruled. I found myself being forcibly dragged inside.

Out of all the games in the arcade, Fumiko decided on a fighting game in a head-to-head cabinet. It was brand-new, and it used the same fighting system *Versus Town* did. Games in head-to-head cabinets were designed so you could either play against the computer or another person in the arcade. The cabinets contained back-to-back screens so you could fight an opponent literally standing opposite you on the other side of the cabinet. The winner of the match got to keep playing, but it was game over for the loser. If the loser wanted to play again, he had to pony up more money. If the loser kept putting in coins, the winner could conceivably keep playing indefinitely. Fighting games were all about the survival of the fittest.

Before the Internet took off, it had been a very profitable

setup. I'd heard of entire arcades filled with nothing but fighting games. Grown men with pockets stuffed full of hundred-yen coins would go to the arcades to meet up with their friends and battle away the hours. Stories like that had captured my imagination as a kid, but before I was old enough to do it myself, the fighting game fad was already a distant memory. Now the arcades had only a handful of fighting games tucked away in the corners, patronized by a steady stream of nostalgic diehards.

I slid a coin into the slot.

Fumiko chose a karateka. She wasn't bad. Under her control, the karateka held its own against the computer. Using different combinations of joystick motions and button presses to execute moves was a difficult concept for the uninitiated to grasp, but it only took Fumiko two or three tries before she was pulling off some of the trickier attacks. Compared to her performance on the crane game, she was a natural.

She had just defeated her second computer opponent when a challenger appeared. He was good. He countered Fumiko's attack, and her karateka sailed into the air. Before the karateka had a chance to plant its feet solidly back on terra firma, its health gauge was at zero.

Fumiko frowned. "What was that?"

"That was a midair combo."

"I figured that much out. What I want to know is why'd he use different attacks in the air than he used on the ground?"

"You noticed? I'm impressed."

"Don't make fun."

"He was watching you to know what counter to use."

"That's impossible."

"People do it all the time. It's like baseball. If a batter can read a pitcher's body language, he can figure out what kind of pitch he's going to throw."

"If it's that easy, why doesn't everyone hit a homerun?"

"Knowing what's coming isn't everything, but it's a start. If you practice, and have a response for anything he might throw at you ready to go in the blink of an eye, then you've got the upper hand."

"Isn't that cheating?"

"The guy who taught me to play said there's no rule against reacting to what you see."

"What happened to 'cheaters never win'?"

"Look out, here comes the next round."

It was a best-of-three match, and Fumiko lost both games in a grand total of twenty seconds. It was hardly a match at all.

"That is *really* frustrating."

"Sure is."

"I wanna go again."

"Fine by me, but you're gonna lose."

"I won't know until I try."

I sighed. There were things I understood that Fumiko didn't. She was a kid who'd just swung a bat for the first time, and now she wanted to go up against the New York Yankees. It might have looked like a fair fight; they both had the same joystick, the same buttons, the same screen. But the gulf of experience between Fumiko and her unseen challenger was wide and unfathomably deep.

Fumiko lost the next match in under thirty seconds. I thought about telling whoever was playing her to go easy, since she was obviously a beginner, but I didn't say anything. She had sat down at a head-to-head game, so if a challenger wanted to wipe the floor with her, there wasn't anything she could do about it. Those were the rules of the RL arcade.

Fumiko rose to her feet in a huff. "It's only a game. So how come I feel so humiliated?"

"Because it's only a game. C'mon, let's go."

"Not so fast. I want revenge." Her eyes gleamed with determination. "This is the kind of game you play, right?"

"Forget it."

"Why?"

"If it means that much to you, you should practice until

you're good enough to get your own revenge."

Fumiko looked up at me with puppy-dog eyes. Apparently I hadn't quite worked off the notebook debt yet. There was only one way out. I sat down at the controls, slid a coin into the slot, and selected the karateka.

I didn't have a grudge against the jujutsuka who challenged Fumiko, and I didn't want to go overboard with her right there, so I only gave the fight about 80 percent. I won the best-of-three match in forty seconds.

I heard a man shout from the other side of the cabinet. Another challenger appeared—an eagle claw. This wasn't the same player who used the jujutsuka against Fumiko.

Eagle claw was a style of gongfu that focused on attacks made with the hand held in a position resembling—you guessed it— the claw of an eagle. They had a wide range of hand techniques at their disposal, and they could easily defeat an opponent in a single flurry of attacks. The eagle claw stylist was one of the most powerful characters in the game.

Using a cancel trick, the eagle claw could access certain secret moves. As it turns out, the arcade version of the game still had some bugs. If you canceled out of a spin attack, you could interrupt the move *after* the game had registered the attack. Since the move was considered canceled, the attacker could go right into his next move. The person on the receiving end, however, faced a recovery time whether he'd blocked the attack or taken the hit, so once the move landed he would take an endless string of hits. People who knew the game called such tricks the Dark Arts, and it was playing dirty.

The eagle claw canceled out of a spin punch and immediately threw, and canceled, a reverse punch. In all of three seconds, my karateka had been knocked out of the ring. I lost the round.

"He kicked your ass."

"Quiet."

I took a deep breath, cleared my head, and concentrated on the screen.

Unlike RL, the rules in computer games were relentlessly rigid. There was no gray area. Sure, the guy sitting on the other side of the cabinet had turned to the Dark Arts, but in a very real way, the bug that made that possible was just another rule. It wasn't a bug, it was a feature. Crying foul wouldn't change a damn thing. If taking one hit meant losing the round, all you had to do was avoid getting hit. I could do that. At least I hoped I could.

I won the next round without a scratch. From behind the cabinet I heard the sound FX of a fist striking the control panel. It didn't bother me. I was the karateka now. My body was nothing more than the CPU controlling it. A CPU didn't get angry. A CPU didn't bring its fist crashing down on the control panel. I won three matches in a row. Six flawless victories. The man sitting on the other side of the cabinet stood up.

There was no expression on his face. A poorly rendered texture was plastered over the polygons that made up his head. Three earrings sparkled in his right ear. His left ear was unadorned. He looked a little taller than me.

"Well? Ain't you got nothin' to say for yourself?"

"Ain't," I answered, not stirring from my seat, "ain't a word. Or didn't you learn anything in school?" A burst of laughter erupted from behind the cabinet. Three Earrings's pal.

"You're startin' to piss me off."

"Only starting? Must be losing my touch."

"You wanna come say that to my face, bitch?"

"Etsuro, don't," Fumiko interjected, twenty minutes too late.

"You should go on home," I said, standing.

Three Earrings, his pal, and I walked out of the arcade. Two against one was hardly a fair fight, but I don't think fair was high on their agenda, and I didn't bother to ask. Most of what happened in RL gave fair a wide berth. The only rules that mattered were the rules of wherever you happened to be, and you could count on each and every person to follow his own interpretation. Right and wrong were in the eye of the beholder, and they were secrets best kept to yourself.

We fought in the back alleys of Shinjuku. An air conditioner was kicking up a racket of a sound FX. I threw a punch and missed. One of them threw a punch and hit. My health gauge went into freefall. Their fists rained down on me so fast I was fairly certain they were using the cancel bug. I gritted my teeth. A knee hit me in the stomach and I rose into the air. Just a bunny hop, really, compared to the graceful arcs traced by a character hit with a counter in *Versus Town*. *This is too easy*, I laughed to myself.

My health gauge dropped to zero.

~

"Are you okay?"

My eyes opened at the sound of Fumiko's voice.

I was lying lengthwise across a rock-hard bench. Fumiko was cradling my head in her lap. She had placed a damp handkerchief over my face. My mouth tasted of iron and blood and cloth. Moving would have required too much effort, so I just lay there with my head in her lap, listening to the sound FX of her beating heart.

"I'm sorry," she said. "It was my fault."

"No, it wasn't you."

"You usually go around picking fights?"

"Actually, that was the first fight I've ever been in."

"Like I said, my fault."

"No, I was asking for it."

It really wasn't Fumiko's fault. There was something deep inside me that had made me take things too far. The sound FX of Three Earrings punching the control panel, something I could never hear an opponent do over the Internet, might have had something to do with it. Truth was, I couldn't explain exactly what had made me do it, so I didn't even try.

"Does it hurt?"

"No more than you'd expect."

"You're bleeding," she said, gently wiping my lips. I felt the heat building in my chest rush out between my teeth.

"A balloon full of blood," I muttered.

"What?"

"Something a friend of mine said once. People are two-thirds water, so we're just a bag of skin with blood sloshing around inside. That's why we bleed when we're hurt."

"You think he's right?"

I closed my eyes. "I dunno." A red balloon drifted through my thoughts.

Around when I started elementary school, my mother took me to a rooftop fair at one of the local department stores. There was a person dressed up in a bear costume. If you beat the bear in a game of rock-paper-scissors, you won a balloon. Not a silvery, Roswell UFO balloon. A shiny, blood-red balloon.

I figured out how to win watching the bear play his first game. His hands were essentially mittens, so he could only throw rock and paper. Watching a few more games, I noticed the bear was delivering rock and paper pretty much fifty-fifty. If it was a tie you got to go again, so as long as you kept throwing out paper, sooner or later you'd win. With a setup like that, you'd have to be a dolt to lose to the bear. Of course the whole point was to keep the kids happy, so I'm sure they had enough on hand to give every kid in the place and his brother a balloon. But to me it didn't seem very sporting to keep throwing out paper against an opponent who could only choose between rock and paper.

When my turn finally came, I went with scissors. The bear played rock. I didn't get a balloon. I had traded a red balloon for my honor. Clenching my six-year-old fist, I watched a balloon bobbing in the proud hand of one of the winners. I didn't regret the choice I made, but it didn't make the taste of loss any less bitter.

I don't think I've changed all that much since then.

"Are you listening?"

"What?"

Fumiko held my head between her palms. "You're so warm." The faint smell of olive blossoms hung in the air.

I opened my eyes. Fumiko was staring down at me with onyx eyes the same jet-black color as her hair. A smile blossomed on her face. "You say some weird things."

"Really? I just say what comes into my head."

"Most people put their thoughts through filter after filter, until they've distilled out all the impurities."

"Why?"

"Because they're weak."

"I don't feel all that strong."

"But you are."

A gentle breeze caressed my cheek. It felt good against my burning skin. I could smell her on that breeze. I couldn't tell whether the air was warm or cool.

"Where are we?" I asked.

"The park near City Hall."

"How'd we get here?"

"You walked on your own two feet." She told me I'd fought with those guys for nearly twenty minutes before the attendant she called broke it up.

"What time is it?"

"Nearly one o'clock."

"Where do you live?"

"Gotanda."

"Then you better hurry."

"What about you?"

"I'll sleep here till morning."

"I can't leave you here like this."

"Maybe not."

The Tōbu Tōjō line had already stopped running, but if Fumiko hurried, she could still make the last train to Gotanda. I let my eyes flutter closed.

A splash sound FX. Something cold on my right hand.

"It's raining." Fumiko must have felt it too.

The skies were clear, but the volume of the *plop plop plop* sound FX rose, the number of drops on my arms keeping pace. Of all the times for it to rain. My mouth twisted into a wry smile.

Fumiko's voice rose above the rain. "We'll be soaked if we stay here."

"It's just a summer rain. It'll pass."

"We should go somewhere. I know a place that stays open until morning."

"I don't feel like sitting."

"Then what should we do?"

"We can sleep here," I offered. "Don't worry, it'll be fine."

There was a long pause before she spoke again. "Then we're not going to do anything?"

"What's there to do?"

"You know…whatever."

"Either way." Not the right answer.

"Try not to care so much."

"Sorry. I'm just tired," I said.

"I know, I know. Sorry."

Another uncomfortable pause. My turn to break it. "Hey, I was wondering. What were you doing in Kabuki-chō tonight?"

"Looking for that cat. You know, the blue one that makes dreams come true."

The conversation with the bat lady came rushing back to me. *You won't have much luck during the day.*

Finding an honor student like Fumiko in a place like Kabuki-chō, after hours no less, didn't make a helluva lot of sense, but the cat thing explained it. Fumiko Nagihara, a girl who searched the RL streets of Kabuki-chō by night for a blue cat, a girl who could flash a disarming hamburger-shop smile, did, in fact, have some interesting quirks lurking just beneath the surface. I didn't believe for a second this blue cat actually existed, but something in me envied the fact that she did.

The two RL thugs who'd given me a complimentary twenty-minute deep tissue massage were just a couple of ordinary punks. They weren't world champions. They were nobodies. There would be no pride, no honor, in training through some power ballad montage to take my revenge on the likes of them. Scouring the virtual world to fight the best of the best was much more appealing. The object of my search didn't exist in RL, with its multitude of lossless-quality sound FX.

I felt Fumiko's gaze on the back of my head as we walked.

One night in a Shinjuku hotel cost nine thousand yen. Enough to pay the subscription to *Versus Town* for ten months. Enough that I'd have to cancel my cell phone and use the money to pay for the game instead. Enough that it hurt. Not enough to make me complain to Fumiko.

CHAPTER 5

I PRESSED THE A BUTTON and became Tetsuo. It was 1:50 in the morning. In Versus Town it was the middle of the day. Tetsuo headed for Sanchōme.

Sanchōme was the sort of place that ordinary people would have associated with the term "virtual reality." There were houses no one lived in, stores with nothing for sale, characters hanging around doing nothing in particular. Shops stood along the road, their shelves lined with cans and boxes that were, in fact, only textures pasted on the polygons of the shelves. The buttons on the vending machines were textures too. You couldn't even push them. There were crosswalks painted on the streets, but not a single car. At least for now, characters in this city existed only to fight.

If the stories were true, Sanchōme was also the stalking ground of the mysterious ganker.

Today's objective: finding the ganker and fighting him. No matter how good he was, Tetsuo should be able to give him a run for his money. Who knows, Tetsuo might even be the first character to beat him. If Tetsuo could beat a character who himself had beaten one of the top four, then Pak, arguably the best and easily the most famous character in Versus Town, was sure to want to fight him. And if Tetsuo could beat Pak, there was no one left to beat. Everyone would know he was the best.

I tapped the stick twice. Tetsuo broke into a run.

Sanchōme was squalid and cluttered. Compared to Main Street, the roads felt tight and claustrophobic. Objects whose purpose I couldn't begin to guess littered the roadside. Tetsuo spent all his time in Itchōme and Nichōme, so he hadn't learned the ins and outs of Sanchōme's virtual world.

I kicked a reddish brown cylinder blocking the road. A clanging sound FX. It must have been a steel drum.

The drum was just the tip of the iceberg. There were metal pipes, cans of kerosene, rocks thrown in for variety, shapes I couldn't make heads or tails of—a truly extravagant display of polygons lay rotting in the streets. Each time I rounded a corner I was greeted by a new piece of debris, making it difficult to run in a straight line. It felt like an RPG dungeon they had turned over to the intern to design. Tetsuo weaved his way through narrow alleyways, dashing from one clump of litter to the next.

In spite of it being midday, the streets of Sanchōme were devoid of other characters. The only signs that anyone was there at all were fleeting glimpses Tetsuo caught of shapes darting out of one building and into another. The buildings themselves were a mix of Western-style houses with facades of woven ivy textures and Japanese houses with polygonal tiles set neatly on their roofs. Some of the houses were clearly occupied, but none had signs declaring to whom they belonged. I wanted to follow the runners and exchange some words, but each time a door flew open, I felt my resolve shrivel.

There was no private property in Versus Town. Tetsuo could go into any of the buildings these characters were darting in and out of. But what you could do and what you should do weren't always the same thing. Sanchōme probably had its own unwritten code of conduct. The thought of invading the privacy of characters Tetsuo had never met before didn't sit too well either.

Still wanting for any specific destination, Tetsuo roamed the mazelike streets. He had been exploring for about thirty minutes when he came across a solitary man who was repeatedly jumping into a wall. His body was wrapped in a deep indigo shinobi outfit, and on his feet he wore a pair of rubber-soled tabi so black they swallowed the light. One look at his stance and I could tell, despite the ninja gear, that he was a lightweight jujutsuka.

The man would start his run at the wall from a distance of about ten steps, springing into the air when only three steps remained between him and the wall. He traced a gently curving parabola as he rose, reaching its apex just before he came in contact with the wall. His jump had come just short of reaching the top. On his current trajectory, he would crash into the wall. In the instant he hung at the pinnacle of his leap, he twisted his body to the side. He had given the command to air-block. The polygons that formed his body caught on the top of the wall. He repeated the air-block command, shifting his center of gravity and sending him slipping down the far side of the wall.

There were several different kinds of wall in Versus Town. There was the wall that surrounded the city, which was impossible to pass through or over. There were walls that anyone could leap over with a simple jump. And then there were walls like the one the jujutsuka was repeatedly jumping, walls that could be overcome with just the right combination of skill and technique.

A short while later the jujutsuka came sailing back over the wall the same way he'd jumped it a few moments before. Then it was back ten steps, run, leap, and air-block all over again. Back and forth, forth and back he jumped over the wall, practicing the way Tetsuo refined his air combos on the wooden dummies in the arena. It seemed Tetsuo had found just the sort of back alley freak who might actually listen to him.

The jujutsuka was making it over the wall about two times out of three. It was a high wall, higher than a middleweight like Tetsuo would have any chance of jumping. The complexity of commands needed to perform a wall jump like this would place it among the most difficult of moves, E-rank all the way.

Tetsuo approached the jujutsuka. I pulled out my keyboard to break the ice.

> Hello.

The jujutsuka canceled out of the dash he'd just begun and turned to face Tetsuo. He stood 45 degrees to Tetsuo's left, three and a half paces away. Just far enough to be out of range of a dash throw. Text bubbled above his head.

> Good day, sir. Fine weather we're having, is it not?

Versus Town wasn't exactly a setting for role-playing. Ignoring his odd choice of words and the fact that the weather was always fine, I replied.

> It is.
> Just so. Here, the sun always shines.
> That it does.

Tetsuo's answer lingered above his head. I was still trying to decide what he should say next when the jujutsuka spoke again.

> Might I be of some service?
> Yeah, about that.
> Alas, I am but a novice who has only begun to walk the warrior's path. Ours would be an ill match.
> I'm not here to duel.
> Then perhaps you should remove your headband, my lord.

He raised his hand to indicate the white headband holding back Tetsuo's hair. It was a skillful and fluid gesture.

When your health dropped to zero anywhere outside the arena, the system forced you to log out. It was a feature designed to keep the city from descending into chaos with brawls on every street corner. When you logged back in, you had to go through the hassle of getting back to wherever you'd been. But this wasn't enough to deter everyone. A faction of players decided that since it was a fighting game, they wanted to fight. They started wearing headbands and wristbands to identify themselves. Before long, the town was neatly divided into two groups, characters who chose to fight anytime, anywhere, and those who fought only in the arena. It was a little bit like gangs showing their colors. At a glance, you could tell where someone stood and know how to approach them.

The white headband encircling Tetsuo's head signaled that he was a top-tier fighter who would accept challenges anywhere in the game. The jujutsuka standing in front of him wore neither headband nor wristband. Unlike Tetsuo, he clearly had no interest in street fighting.

> Of late, danger has come even here to Sanchōme. People have grown obsessed with farcical duels. Alas, I can scarcely scale a wall in peace.
> I thought fighting was the whole point.
> The point is what you make of it. I'll not deny that many choose to make dueling that point, but dueling in and of itself has no more or less meaning than jumping walls.

He had worked out quite a little philosophy for himself, but we were starting to stray off-topic.

> I'm not here to duel. I'm looking for someone.

The jujutsuka relaxed his stance.

> And who might that be?
> Have you heard about the snake boxer?
> Snake boxer?
> They say he hangs out somewhere around here.
> This place teems with eagles and snakes. They're two of

the best schools, as you must surely know.
> The snake I'm looking for is no ordinary snake.
> An extraordinary snake, then?
> Extraordinary enough to beat 963. One of the top four.
> Ah, then it is Jack whom you seek.
> Jack?
> The shadow who stalks Sanchōme.
> That's the guy.
> Here he is known as Ganker Jack.

The jujutsuka folded his arms. The shadow of the wall that towered over us lay unmoving at our feet.

~

The web of roads and alleyways grew more and more complex the further I went.

After he had parted ways with the jujutsuka, Tetsuo had gone back toward the outskirts of Sanchōme. According to his new friend, there was a saloon in Versus Town where people went to swap stories about the comings and goings in the virtual city. If I wanted to hear more about Ganker Jack, he assured me, there was no surer place to go.

I tilted the stick gently up and to the right. Tetsuo hopped over a log blocking the middle of the street. There was much more to Sanchōme than I had imagined. Houses, one very much like the next, lined long, winding streets. A passage that, at a distance, seemed nothing more than an alley barely wide enough for a person to pass could lead to vast, empty courtyards. And not a single character appeared to break the emptiness.

I'd heard European cities from the Middle Ages were rife with blind alleys and dogleg roads. They actually designed the cities to be difficult to navigate as a defense against invasion. Sanchōme appeared to be built on the same premise. Its tangled skein of roads and byways seemed tailor-made to prevent the uninitiated from penetrating its veil. Each new road looked very much like the last. It was as though the saloon was not *meant* to be found.

By the time I finally did find it, ten minutes had passed since I left the jujutsuka. Even coming straight from Itchōme it would probably take fifteen minutes to get here.

Tetsuo stood in front of the bar. The place looked like something out of a spaghetti Western. The walls were covered with textures of weather-beaten wood. The only entrance was a pair of swinging doors. Nearby, a lone wooden barrel stood sentry. Above the entrance, an old sign rested atop two massive beams. The polygons of the sign were just crooked enough to draw attention to themselves. Unlike RL, in a virtual world you had to go out of your way to make anything that wasn't perfectly parallel with everything else. JTS SALOON declared the sign in giant letters. The only thing missing was a good whinny sound FX.

Tetsuo pushed the swinging doors open and peered in.

Inside was murky and dim. Two characters stood in front of the bar, having a conversation. There were probably others further back in the room, but it was too dark to be sure. Maybe staring at the sunlit cityscape for so long just made the saloon seem darker than it was.

I gave the stick two quick taps, then brought it back to neutral. Tetsuo speed-dashed into the saloon.

> Howdy, pardner.

The man who spoke was a heavyweight fighter behind the counter. The classic bartender.

There was no concept of money in *Versus Town*. Unlike role-playing games, fighting games didn't have rare items or experience points. So it surprised me to see a bartender controlled by a real person.

One by one, the text bubbles over the heads of the other characters in the dim cavern of the bar faded. I could feel the eyes of everyone in the room move to Tetsuo. The characters were as still as statues. The textures that passed for their eyes stared blankly. But all across RL, over mile after mile of network cable, the players were watching every move of this newcomer on their television screens.

Tetsuo turned toward the bartender.

> I'm looking for someone.
> This here's a bar, son.
> Huh?
> You gotta order somethin'.
> I don't have any money.
> Don't need no money. So what'll it be? We got whisky-and-water, bottled beer, and mineral water. Them's the only three drinks on offer.
> Gimme a mineral water, then.
> Comin' right up.

The bartender slammed down the glass, generating a loud *clink* sound FX. I input a complex command and Tetsuo extended his hand above the counter. I had seen the command in the manual but never used it until now. Tetsuo failed to grasp the glass on his first two attempts. In the process, I managed to send the polygonal glass rolling along the countertop. The glass emitted a gravelly rumble sound FX as it moved, but not a drop of its contents spilled. Not so much as a ripple disturbed the surface of the transparent substance filling the glass. The water in Versus Town was just a mass of polygons rendered using matrix calculus. You could drop a crystal glass on the floor and it wouldn't break.

> You new?

The woman had waited for Tetsuo to pick up the glass before approaching him.

> I've had my account a little over a month.
> This your first time here?
> Yeah, you could say that.

She was wearing a skin-tight purple suit with high heels to match. Her hair was long and black. A lightweight. Drunken fist. The sake bottle hanging from her hip clashed horribly with the suit, but if she hadn't been made of polygons, she wouldn't have looked half-bad.

People said the person who played Keith, one of the top four, was actually some high school girl. But just because a character spoke like a woman didn't necessarily mean the player was female. In fact, most of the time it probably wasn't. The ratio of male-to-female accounts in *Versus Town* was nine-to-one.

> I'm looking for someone. Maybe you've heard of him.
> What's his name?
> Ganker Jack.
> You too, huh?
> There are other people looking for him?
> Plenty.

She gave an exaggerated shrug. The fact that she'd chosen to play a drunken fist spoke well of her skill. She continued.

> Seems like everyone is talking about him these days. It's getting a little old.
> Do you know anyone who's seen him?
> Hard to say. I couldn't care less, personally. Hashimoto's the person to ask, but he isn't here today.
> Too bad.
> It's a pain in the ass is what it is. We haven't seen 963 since

Jack beat him, and the hardcore keep hanging around.

> 963 used to come here?

> Not just him. Pak and Keith drop by sometimes. Tanaka's the only one of the top four who never comes. But he's always been hardcore.

> What's all this hardcore stuff?

> Just the way it sounds.

Before she could continue, a man with long hair broke into the conversation.

> You're wasting your breath on that one, Masumi.

He was wearing a light brown vest over a white shirt with a raised collar. An intricate pattern decorated his boots, which reached to just below his knees. His hair matched the color of his vest, and he wore it parted down the middle of his head. He was a middleweight snake boxer, and he had on a black wristband. A streetfighter like Tetsuo.

He caught the leg of a nearby chair with a middle foot sweep, pulling it close enough for him to sit down and cross his legs.

> Listen up, scrub. You wanna fight, you go down to the arena. You got no business here.

A mischievous grin was plastered across his face. There were no commands to change your expression, so that meant wherever he went he wore the same ridiculous smile. Maybe he thought it made him look like some kind of twisted nihilist, but it looked pretty stupid to me.

Tetsuo dropped into a fighting stance.

> Who the hell do you think you are?

> Ricky.

> I'm
> I don't give a rat's ass about the name of some scrub who does a speed dash inside a bar. Running indoors is for dogs and children too young to know better.
> You looking for a fight?
> I'd say I'm finding one.
> Leave the new guy alone, Ricky.

That last was Masumi, butting in.

> That tournament's bringing these guys out of the wood-work. I bet this one thinks he's got the brass to take on the top four.
> I'm just here looking for Jack.
> To fight him, I know. You really want a fight, go to an arcade. You can find Pak out in Shinjuku.
> At an arcade?
> Don't make me type it twice. A-R-C-A-D-E
> That's a little behind the times, isn't it?
> You just don't get it, do you? Times may change, but holy ground is holy ground.

Pak was the best player in Versus Town. In RL, he was an editor for a video game magazine. Even I had heard the stories about him showing up in arcades on Kokusai-dōri on the weekends. One of the many pilgrims to the "holy ground" that was the arcades of Shinjuku.

But all that was a decade ago, long before the Internet had taken root. It used to be, people who lived in Mizuhodai could only play against other people who lived in Mizuhodai. If they didn't like it, they could hop on a train to take them to Shinjuku. That was all well and good for people who lived in Mizuhodai. Saitama Prefecture wasn't especially far from Tokyo. But if you lived in Hokkaido or Kyushu, it was a different story. There weren't a lot of people who could afford to catch a bullet train to Tokyo just to ride out and play some games. Now, thanks to the Internet, the best players in the world were only as far away as your television. You could play your neighbor, you could play people in Hokkaido and Kyushu, you could even play people in the United States. Earth was a tiny place as far as the light pushing those packets back and forth was concerned. Nobody needed the rickety old arcade that shook every time the Tōbu Tōjō line passed by overhead anymore. This was the first time I'd heard anyone suggest that an arcade was the place you had to go if you were serious about playing. Why should anyone have to resort to going to a real city in RL to accomplish something you could do online?

Ricky the snake boxer waved his hand. The gesture had already gotten on my nerves.

> Pak never fights here.

Ricky stood before continuing.

> You're not as good as you think. You think you're some kind of wolf, a real leader of the pack. But you're just another pig to the slaughter.
> What did you call me?
> You forget how to read? I said you were a pig.
> You want to take this outside?
> Thought you'd never ask.

Tetsuo and Ricky walked out of the bar, one after the other. Behind them, I could see Masumi shrug one last time at the edge of the screen.

We stood facing each other in the street in front of the saloon. Half the characters inside came spilling out through the swinging doors to watch the fight. It was Ricky who spoke.

> Whenever you're ready.

The two characters stood exactly five steps apart.

Snake boxing, or *shéquán*, is a Chinese martial art named for its trademark serpentine movements. When the developers were laying the foundation for *Versus Town*, they called in a famous Hong Kong movie star to do all the motion capture for the game. Apparently the guy had played a snake fist stylist in one of his movies. Along with eagle claw, it was one of the most powerful schools in the game.

I counted slowly to three before inputting the speed-dash command. Tetsuo rushed forward and threw his fastest punch. Ricky dodged the punch with a crouching back dash. I pressed the A button to cancel out of the kick I'd already buffered. Move. Block. Tetsuo crouched as he moved forward and to the right, girding himself against low attacks. Ricky moved at an angle, tracking Tetsuo's path. They spun 60 degrees, always facing each other.

So long as he was crouching, high punches and kicks would sail right over Ricky's head. You had to be able to reach your opponent's back to throw him, so doing a kick-cancel throw was out too. Ricky had dodged Tetsuo's punch in the most effective way possible. If Tetsuo had kept attacking, more likely than not he would have taken a counterhit.

My knuckles whitened as they gripped the stick. Ricky made his move.

His left hand darted forward in a middle punch. Cancel. Low kick. Back-dash to the left. Ricky swung 120 degrees to Tetsuo's left. I had managed to dodge the middle punch, but the low kick hit home. Tetsuo's health dropped by a fraction.

I maneuvered Tetsuo forward and to the right, keeping Ricky directly in front of him. I launched a forward middle kick, but Ricky spun away back and to the left again.

Tetsuo speed-dashed forward. As he ran in, Ricky caught him with a crouching punch. Another sliver off Tetsuo's health. I backed him away. Tetsuo's counterattack bit at air. While Tetsuo was recovering from the attack, Ricky moved in.

I gave the command for a throw break. Ricky heaved Tetsuo onto his shoulder, just as I had expected. The throw break I'd already buffered sent Tetsuo somersaulting over Ricky's head to land safely on the ground. Both characters back-dashed.

Ricky would feint an approach, then back away, constantly circling Tetsuo. Tetsuo kept up his attacks, but they all seemed to fall just a few pixels short. Ricky was avoiding any decisive moves, favoring weak but reliable attacks instead. He was bleeding out Tetsuo's health one drop at a time. Tetsuo specialized in midair combos initiated along with a counter, which put him at a disadvantage when facing an opponent who kept his guard up and played everything close to the vest. This was going to be a tough fight.

A crowd of characters thronged the narrow space in front of the saloon. Row upon row of infinitely thin polygonal text bubbles floated in the air.

> Kick his ass!
> Don't encourage them.
> Picking on scrubs can't be good for your karma.
> Up with wolves, down with pigs!
> Outta the way! I can't see!
> I think he fell asleep.
> Who is this asshat, anyway?
> Who cares? More fuel for the fire.
> Good luck burning this place down.
> I could teach you a thing or two.
> Ugh, come on already!

Bastards. They could type whatever they wanted. My hands were glued to the controls, and in this particular virtual world your hands were your mouth. If you couldn't reach your keyboard, you were a mute.

Tetsuo advanced in silence. Ricky spun to the left. Tracking him as he moved, Tetsuo threw back-to-back punches—a left, then a right. Neither landed. Ricky dodged with a back dash. Instinctively, I canceled out of the second punch and did a speed dash. Ricky was still mid-move, and Tetsuo was right on top of him. Tetsuo made a low sweep kick. Knowing it would send Ricky tumbling to the ground, I buffered my next attack.

Tetsuo's kick never connected. One of the beams holding up the saloon sign blocked his foot. I hadn't accounted for the terrain. Things like this didn't happen in the arena.

The impact left Tetsuo tottering off-balance. Ricky dashed forward and delivered a sharp open-palmed strike. The sound FX of the counterhit rang in my ears. Tetsuo's body soared into the air.

As Tetsuo hung suspended in the air, Ricky delivered one punch, then another. Canceling, he struck again with his elbow and followed up with a crouching punch. Tetsuo was on the ground now, but instead of pressing the attack, Ricky stepped back, putting some distance between them. Text bubbled over his head.

> Quit foolin' around.

While he waited for Tetsuo to regain his feet, Ricky made a show of brushing the dust off his clothes. He still wore the same grin he'd had inside the saloon. Once that texture had been chosen, there was no going back without redesigning one's whole character.

The characters' polygonal bodies moved with extreme fidelity. When they punched, they extended their arms and drew them back. When they kicked, the same was true of their legs. A hit that landed as a character was drawing in his arms or legs was considered a counter. Counters sent characters flying high into the air. Dealing massive damage to a character soaring helplessly across the screen was one of the core strategies of the game.

Given split-second timing, people don't have the luxury

to think over what they're going to do. Our bodies react on their own with the action they're most familiar with. A conditioned reflex. To hone those reflexes, martial artists practice thousands of strikes a day, astronauts run through the same simulations over and over, and I practice my combos on the training dummy. There is no element of chance when you're up against other players in a virtual world. A good player only wins as often as he deserves to win. I had proven that at the arcade in Shinjuku.

As soon as Tetsuo stood, he dashed forward to close the gap between himself and Ricky. Ricky backed off and to the right.

Tetsuo threw a middle punch. Ricky blocked. I canceled the kick I'd buffered after the punch and made a low kick instead. Ricky back dashed. I jumped and threw a middle punch from the air, immediately followed by a high spin kick. Ricky avoided both attacks with a crouching back dash. Tetsuo canceled out of the spin kick. This wasn't getting him anywhere.

Tetsuo was waiting for Ricky's next crouching back dash. Timed right, he should be able to land a counterattack. Tetsuo rushed forward, sticking his knee out in Ricky's path.

Only, Ricky wasn't there. Tetsuo's knee sliced through thin air. Impossible. As Ricky spun to the left, his knee struck Tetsuo. The counterhit sound FX played.

Once more, Tetsuo's body rose into the air. Ricky punched, canceled, and punched again. Tetsuo went crashing into, then bouncing off, the polygonal barrel. Ricky caught him with an open-palmed thrust as he rebounded off the barrel. Ricky dashed forward, canceled, punched, and punched again. A spinning roundhouse kick provided the coup de grace.

Tetsuo's lifeless body collapsed across the barrel, jittering as it grated slowly to the ground. A gray web spread across the screen. One final bubble of text flickered over Ricky's head.

> Yup. Bacon.

The system booted Tetsuo offline.

The screen changed to a uniform shade of blue. A tiny message swam in the center of the screen.

WOULD YOU LIKE TO LOG BACK IN?

I slammed the controller onto the floor. A dull pain rose in my thumb; I'd hit the floor hard enough to split my thumbnail. Blood black as ink welled up from beneath the nail.

I sucked on my wounded thumb. A bitter, metallic taste filled my mouth.

Tonight's score: 0 wins, 1 loss.

CHAPTER 6

A TEPID MIASMA HUNG OVER THE CAMPUS during the rainy season. The weather seemed permanently stuck in an obscene limbo between blistering heat and pouring rain. The humidity in the air made it an effort to breathe. Shinjuku felt like a giant steam cooker. The flame beneath the pot had just been lit, and it would only get worse from here.

Fumiko Nagihara and I were in the same year and in the same department, so naturally we had the same required courses. Whenever I attended any given class, there was approximately a 70 percent chance she would be there. Fumiko was on campus every day except Sunday.

Fumiko hated it when anyone used her last name. She said she didn't like the way it sounded. She had an aversion to the usual nicknames too. I think her girlfriends called her Fumi, or Fumi-chan, but I wasn't about to go there. Instead, I played it safe by addressing her by name as little as humanly possible.

I'd made it to class the last Thursday, Friday, and even Saturday. Fumiko complained about the rain. Apparently the front had stalled right over the city. My surge in attendance left me with more cards than I knew what to do with. I understood why the students who showed up for every class didn't bother collecting cards. They'd end up with enough to build a deck.

Somehow we'd reached an unspoken agreement that we would sit together in the seats along the wall seven rows from the front of the classroom. Fumiko didn't like it when I had my headphones on, so I did my best to listen to the lecture instead.

The sound FX of a desk squeaking on the floor. The sound FX of Fumiko breathing. The sound FX of the air passing through my windpipe. A wealth of discordant sounds always filled the classrooms.

Fumiko turned to me when class ended.

"Why don't you ever talk about your family?"

"There's nothing to say."

"Really?"

"Really."

"I've heard people have more intimate conversations when they're talking to someone they look up to." She stared at me meaningfully. "With everyone else, their conversations are just filler. At least that's how it's supposed to work for girls."

My family was an ordinary family. There must have been thousands of families just like ours scattered across Japan. I didn't have any complaints about my parents, and as far as I knew, they didn't have any about me. If I took another half step into the virtual world, I risked being pulled in the way my friend who'd vanished into the northern wastes had. But so far, I'd managed to keep my feet planted firmly in RL, albeit on the borders. There just wasn't all that much about RL that I felt needed discussing.

Fumiko forged ahead. "What are you interested in? What are your hobbies?"

"Games."

"But you don't go to arcades, I know that. You have a PlayStation or something?"

The PlayStation wasn't exactly cutting-edge technology anymore, but explaining that to Fumiko would have been more trouble than it was worth.

"That's right."

"Anything else?"

"Nope."

Clearly Fumiko wasn't satisfied. "What about that?" She pointed.

"It's a dried flower."

"So that's another hobby of yours?"

"Yeah, I guess. I like to read, watch movies…You know, the

usual." To me, a hobby was something you only had one of, but I didn't feel like explaining that either.

"I don't think I'd call those hobbies."

"Why not?"

"I don't know. Aren't those things all boys do as kids?"

"Sure, but there's nothing saying you have to stop when you grow up. Didn't the president of Hudson Soft have a miniature train running through his R&D division?"

"That's not a fact I would use to form the cornerstone of an argument," she said.

"Probably not."

Fumiko sighed.

There was no denying that games were entertainment. What set this particular form of entertainment apart from all the others that had come before was a very smart black box called a computer. Games were a doorway that let players step into a make-believe world with its own set of rules. Computers ruled over these imaginary lands as enlightened despots applying the rules with total impartiality and unflagging faithfulness. I think that sense of a protected environment was part of what drew us to games in the first place.

"Are you bored with school?" she asked.

"What makes you think I'm bored?"

"Why else would you ride trains all the way to Shinjuku and never show up for class?" She paused for emphasis. "And you aren't in any clubs, either."

I considered for a moment. I'd thought a lot of things about school, but boring wasn't one of them. "I think it must be the noise."

"What's that supposed to mean?"

"The wind. The cars. Doors closing. Dogs barking. People."

"You're a poet."

"No. No, really. I'm not." Fumiko tilted her head at me. A tiny ear peeked out from beneath her short jet-black bob. The fluorescent lights tinted the moss green of her jacket a vivid hue.

"Every place has its own rhythm," I said.

"I don't understand."

"You don't need to understand."

"Is that so?"

"Maybe I should ask you why you always come to class instead."

"Do I need a reason?"

"I do."

She placed a finger against her lips. "I can't really say. Both of my brothers graduated from college, so I guess I thought I should too. As long as I'm here, I might as well study."

"Hmph."

"You're laughing at me."

"No I'm not," I said.

"You think it's stupid to go to all your classes?"

"No, I don't."

"Then why'd you laugh? And don't tell me that wasn't a laugh. I know what I heard." On some level Fumiko was clearly enjoying this.

The sounds of the classroom felt distant to me, the way they always did. Someone sat in one of the seats behind us. The buttons on his jacket made rattling sound FX as they brushed against the desk.

"Where do you ride?" I blurted.

The question came out of nowhere, surprising even me.

"Ride what?"

"The train."

"You mean which car?"

"No, inside the car."

Fumiko's brow wrinkled in thought. "If there's an open seat, I take it. Middle seat, end seat—doesn't matter. The seats are always heated in the winter. I like that. Do I need a reason for that too?"

"Not really."

Fumiko had graduated from a private high school. Her father

was a banker. She was straitlaced and meticulous, the sort of girl who read back over her own notes to highlight the really important parts in yellow. An honor student who never missed a class. She could walk on the sacred ground of the salarymen and sit in their precious RL seats without arousing even a murmur of protest.

"I'm not the only one here with weird hobbies," I said with a grin.

"Huh?"

"Cat hunting. Or have you given up on that?"

She averted her eyes. "I'm still looking."

"Alone?" I asked. She nodded but said nothing. "Why?"

"Maybe I should quit."

"You don't want to tell me the reason?"

"There is no reason. If it's a hobby, then I don't need one, do I?" She wasn't looking for an answer. She'd made up her mind.

"Okay."

"Will you help me look?"

The two of us were even. All debts paid. Searching the city for a dubious cat from an urban legend wasn't the sort of thing college students were meant to spend their time doing. And my own virtual search for Ganker Jack had encountered problems of its own.

Despite all that, the thought of Fumiko walking alone at night through Kabuki-chō didn't sit well with me. It was like watching a newborn kitten play along the edge of a busy street. I wanted to tell her I'd rather do something—anything—else. But I didn't.

~

One of my classmates in elementary school was convinced that aliens were visiting Earth. I think he must have gotten the notion from some tabloid-style documentary he saw on television. None of us took it very seriously, but he had fallen for it hook, line, and sinker. He'd always been gullible that way.

For a precocious kid who knew he had a 100 percent chance to win if he used paper but had the balls to go fifty-fifty with scissors to keep the game fair, it was obvious that the show was just some grown-up's idea of entertainment. I didn't believe in aliens for a minute. But I still remember how painful it was watching the poor guy searching so earnestly for the aliens the rest of us knew he'd never find.

Compared to that, a blue cat that made dreams come true was a mystery I could live with. It didn't hurt anyone, and if it kept a couple of college students with too much time on their hands entertained, then why not? It was probably just like the bat lady said: some drunk bought paint at a hardware store, applied it to an unfortunate stray, and *voilà*, instant magic cat. I couldn't say much about the dreams coming true bit, but there were stranger things than finding a blue cat in Shinjuku. As adventures went, it was probably less indicative of a deep-seated mental disorder than, say, searching the streets of a virtual world trying to hunt down a mystery assassin probably controlled by some kid from who-knows-where.

A search of the Internet had revealed that there was a notorious black cat known to lurk in Ikebukuro—four stops from Shinjuku on the Yamanote Line—but not our blue one. Apparently someone had been drawing this black cat in obscure places along walls or on lampposts.

When I suggested that Shinjuku's blue cat might be the same sort of prank, Fumiko exploded. Not mysterious enough, I guess. To me, the notion of someone secretly painting black cats all over the city seemed far more romantic, but I didn't want to think how Fumiko might have reacted to that opinion.

After that, I fell into a new routine. Each day I rode a packed train to school and listened to endless lectures that for the most part went in one ear and out the other. Then after class ended and the sun began to sink behind the buildings, I set off into the streets of Shinjuku. To be honest, I could have done without the lectures, but it pissed Fumiko off when I didn't show up for class.

The humid June wind sapped my health like a crouching punch, while the crowded trains were a midair combo that finished the job. I was walking around on empty. Summer was knocking on Shinjuku's door in earnest now. When the front currently lingering over western Japan finally blew through, it would be upon us. The weather man on NHK said that the summer was going to be a particularly hot one. A real scorcher. The warm air pressed down on my exposed skin as though to wring out what little energy I had left.

With a map I'd downloaded off the net in one hand, Fumiko and I walked Shinjuku's streets. A treasure hunt was pretty much the same in the virtual world and the real one. All you had to do was print out a map on graph paper and mark off the squares you'd already checked. Only a thorough search would turn up every last hidden passageway and secret treasure chest. Unlike the virtual world, there were lots of places you couldn't go in RL, at least not legally, and there was no guarantee of finding the key that would let you in. On the upside, there were no illusory walls that could only be breached by finding hidden magic passages, and you wouldn't end up walking in place because you were snagged by a wayward polygon. RL had some things going for it still.

If you believed the ghost theory, we were on a wild goose chase. Avoiding Fumiko's eye, I even checked the bases of lamp-posts and the corners of walls for painted blue cats, but found nothing. I was nearing the point where I would have snuck out early one morning while the city was still sleeping and drawn one myself if I'd only had a single artistic bone in my body.

We had been walking more than three hours straight when we finally took a break at a coffee shop. I was exhausted.

Fumiko was wearing a Naples yellow blouse, the same one she'd had on the day we first met. She wore stretch pants a shade darker. Her silver-rimmed glasses were perched on her nose.

Fumiko examined my face. "You look like the Hustler."

"The what?"

"You know, the movie? Haven't you seen it?"

I searched my memory. It sounded familiar. I think I caught it on some Saturday night television special. The lead was a good-looking guy who played a mean game of pool. "Was that the one with Tom Cruise?"

"No, that was the sequel, *The Color of Money*. I was talking about Paul Newman in *The Hustler*."

"Who's Paul Newman?"

"The guy who taught Tom Cruise how to play pool. Don't you remember?"

"Not ringing any bells."

"So you know all about some CEO who has a train running through his office, but you've never heard of Paul Newman?" She shook her head. "You should watch it. It's really good."

"Maybe I will." I took a swallow of black Guatemalan coffee. "What made you think of *The Hustler*, anyway?"

"You look like him." She shrugged.

The Hustler was a story about a young pool player named Fast Eddie whose dream was to beat pool legend Minnesota Fats. He didn't care about anything else. His friends, his girlfriend… he sacrificed everything for pool. And apparently this was who I reminded Fumiko of.

"It's all in your head."

"I don't think so."

"Whatever."

I didn't know what Paul Newman looked like, but I figured it was a safe bet he was a pretty boy like Tom Cruise. I was no movie star, so whatever it was we had in common, it couldn't have been good looks.

"You like that blouse?"

Fumiko gulped down a swallow of coffee. "What, you don't think it looks good on me?"

"No, it looks great. It's the one you were wearing the day

we met, isn't it?"

A smile rose to her lips. That hamburger-shop smile. The artificial light shining through the window brought out the outline of her bra beneath the yellow fabric. I blinked.

"It's finally summer," Fumiko mused.

"You can say that again."

"You mind coming shopping with me?" She had finished all but the last centimeter of her iced coffee.

"Sure. When?"

"Now."

"What happened to the cat hunt?"

"I never thought I'd hear you worrying about what happened to the cat hunt."

"It's never good to lose sight of your goals."

"You know this from experience?"

"I do."

I took a deep breath—the air was as thick as cotton candy—and cast a questioning glance in Fumiko's direction. She feigned a moment of introspection.

"Don't think this means we're done searching for that cat. Once my mind is made up, it's made up." She grabbed the strap on my bag and started walking. "One other thing," she said without looking back. "This isn't the blouse I was wearing the day we met."

After an exhaustive search, the only purchase Fumiko had to show for her efforts were five gray-striped wooden buttons. We made plans to go see a movie together. I even promised to treat her to dinner in Ebisu. Since she lived in Gotanda, she knew her way around Shinjuku a little better than I did. By the time we went our separate ways at the station, it had been four hours since the sun had set.

Without a soundtrack playing in the background, the world bustled with sound FX, but they were distant and muffled in my ears. The voices rising from the sea of people breaking around us, Fumiko's voice, my own—they all had the same raspy quality, like recordings made on old analog tape.

~

It was Tuesday, twelve past ten in the morning.

Fumiko and I were in our sociology class. The skies above Shinjuku were overcast again. There was an undercurrent of chill on the damp air. A thousand motes of dust danced in bands of light that shone through gaps in the clouds.

We sat side by side in the seventh row from the front of the lecture theater. A professor with thinning hair passed down the aisle beside our desk. He didn't have a comb-over, but there was a distinct seaweed quality to his hair. I recognized that seaweed.

"What's his name?"

"Uemura," she whispered, opening her college-ruled notebook. I didn't even have loose-leaf paper or writing implements in front of me.

"I thought Uemura taught logic?"

"They're brothers."

"No way."

"They are."

I took another look. He was a little shorter than me. The early stages of a pot belly were making themselves known, and his hair was thinning. He wore dark brown sandals and a drab olive necktie. Chalk dust marred his navy blue suit, threadbare from years of harsh dry-cleaning chemicals. In *Versus Town*, he'd be a middleweight. He didn't look all that dissimilar from logic's Professor Uemura.

"He the older brother?"

"Try again."

"The years have not been kind."

"He's had it rough. His brother's a full professor, but he's still just an associate."

"Well, you're certainly up on your trivia."

"You're probably the only person in the room who doesn't

know." Fumiko took out her silver-rimmed glasses.

Once the lecture started, Fumiko didn't say a word. I divided my attention between Uemura the Younger and the fluorescent lights. Today he was off on another topic that seemed inappropriate for a college lecture.

According to Uemura the Younger, cults and con men had merged to create an entirely new business model. Traditionally, cults were exclusive groups that espoused heretical faiths, but there was no particular reason to limit the term to religious groups. You could have a small group of people who believed in the protective powers of rabbits' feet, and the dynamics would remain the same. The members of these tight groups bonded and their interactions with each other became less complicated. In short order, this fostered a sense of fulfillment and solidarity. Con men running pyramid schemes used this solidarity to dupe young, impressionable kids into joining. That was how they got members.

Since younger members of society have no responsibility for their own materialistic lifestyles, they tend to be uniquely idealistic. They represent the societal and political values of the age in which they live.

Following the war, the student movement of the 1960s and '70s was closely related to Japan's economic growth. During the reconstruction, they called for peace, independence, and democracy. At the height of the Cold War, they argued back and forth over communism and capitalism. In the social upheaval that followed, the student movement collapsed due to infighting.

Today's youth, continued Uemura the Younger, had been born into a world without heroes. In the past, heroes gave the young generations something to look up to, to emulate. Now common men stood in their place, and while some among us might approach the status of a hero, there were no more living legends, and thus the young grew up knowing they would never become heroes themselves.

Ironic, then, that man was a creature that inherently aspired toward heroism. A creature that searched for some greater purpose to give meaning to his life. A creature that formed social groups to share their common aspirations. In a developed society, the success of cultlike groups was a foregone conclusion.

There was a cult element even to the companies that created virtual worlds. They provided a shared secret language that outsiders couldn't understand, a place where the young could experience a sense of safety. That was the way of the world. The fads of today's youth were the end product of a society that demanded a cult culture. So sayeth Uemura the Younger.

I shifted my gaze from the blackboard to my side. Fumiko was taking notes. She might have been doing it just to get a rise out of me.

I scratched my head. There was no theory to explain gaming. There was no set of principles, no moral stance that drove you to practice difficult moves. No one stepped into a virtual world for a sense of solidarity. Your opponent on the other end of the network wasn't your friend, your lover, or comrade-in-arms. The only part of them I saw was the character on the screen, and that was all they saw of me. If virtual worlds weren't like that, my friend would never have disappeared into the north.

I learned something from Uemura the Younger that day. University was nothing but talk. I also remembered something very important. Whatever my loss to Ricky had knocked loose snapped back into place with a click so loud I was surprised half the class didn't turn around to look at me. I could feel wheels starting to turn in my head. At that moment, university was not the place I needed to be.

Nor was it any time to be searching for blue cats. Sure, that still had its place. There was no reason I couldn't keep seeing Fumiko in RL. But that was just a distraction to my true purpose. I had a snake boxer to hunt. If I let him slip through my fingers, finding the blue cat wouldn't bring him back. I had a score to settle in the virtual world, and there was nowhere else to do it.

There were people who gave themselves over to addiction, who let themselves lose contact with RL. A risk I was willing to take. I had to go back.

The sound FX died away.

A veil lowered over my field of vision. Fumiko was still taking notes. I stood, noisily hefting my bag onto my shoulder.

"What is it?" she asked.

"I just remembered something I have to do. Gotta run."

"It's the middle of the lecture."

"Sorry."

My legs carried me quickly out of the room. At home, a virtual world was waiting for me.

CHAPTER 7

I PRESSED THE [A] BUTTON. Tetsuo came to Versus Town again, unreal turquoise blue sky, unchanging butter roll clouds, grainy-textured backgrounds and all.

White headband trailing in a digital wind, Tetsuo ran down the right side of Main Street. It was 8:45 PM, more than two hours earlier than he usually arrived. The city still slept.

Versus Town Networks, Inc., was open for business twenty-four hours a day. Players could log in whenever they wanted and stay online for as long as they liked. If you had Internet access and a game console, you could play the game from anywhere in the world. Day and night had no meaning here; the same blue sky was waiting whenever you logged in.

Time in Versus Town trailed RL by half a day. From six o'clock in the morning until noon, the place was a ghost town. The back alleys, Main Street, the arena...all were empty. In the afternoon, kids would start popping up one by one as they came home from school. People who worked during the week showed up between nine PM and midnight.

Up until midnight, the servers were usually running at maximum capacity, so lag was common as they struggled to keep up with all the information that needed to be processed. Fighting the congestion was more trouble than it was worth. For whatever reason, the people who played at this time of day were, by and large, not very good. The best players waited until the mere mortals had gone to sleep before logging in. The city's true potential was only realized after midnight. When the witching hour had come and gone, the number of players dropped off, but there were always a few diehards who stayed online until morning. On a normal day, Tetsuo wouldn't be caught dead showing up before eleven PM.

Tetsuo turned off Main Street into an alleyway. He rounded a corner and sprang over a metal drum liberally decorated with rust spot textures. He weaved his way through the narrow gaps separating the houses. His destination: the JTS Saloon.

The saloon was just as he'd left it. The old sign hung at the same crooked angle. The beam that caught his sweep kick stood just as it had. The walls were textured with the same weather-beaten planks. Still just a horse whinny sound FX away from a spaghetti Western.

Tetsuo walked slowly around the exterior of the saloon. The ground in Sanchōme was uneven and bumpy. When Tetsuo stepped into a depression, his body sank. When he moved over a small mound, he stood a little taller.

As Tetsuo walked, I replayed the fight against Ricky in my head. *Back dash from the column my kick had struck. Back and to the right, then another back dash. A slight move forward by Ricky as he attacked, then a crouching back dash.* I moved Tetsuo just as I'd moved him in the fight. When I was done, I noticed a small hollow in the ground directly in front of where he stood—the exact spot of ground Ricky had held during the fight.

A light, tan-colored texture sprinkled with gravel covered the ground. The shadow of the column in front of the saloon fell just at Tetsuo's feet. The gravel-strewn ground dovetailed perfectly with the Old World feel of Sanchōme. The hollow was deep, but unless you were watching for it, you'd never have noticed Tetsuo's height drop as he stepped into it. No wonder his knee-jab had missed.

As a general rule, characters that held the high ground were at an advantage. Characters who found themselves in midair over a depression or low area took longer to hit the ground, which meant they were vulnerable to that many more attacks while airborne. And of course the opposite was true of characters hit over high ground: they landed sooner, exposing them to fewer attacks in the air. Midair combos dealt massive damage and could easily decide a fight, so holding the high ground was key.

But the high ground came at a price. Since your arm needed to be able to reach behind your opponent to throw him, you had to get much closer to throw. The character who held the high ground also had a more difficult time landing normal hits on his opponent. A low sweep kick could miss because of the downward angle, and it wasn't uncommon for attacks from a higher elevation to sail right over a crouching opponent's head. Essentially, this was what had happened in Tetsuo's fight against Ricky. The best way to handle the situation was to jump over your opponent and use moves that struck down from above, but you had to know what you were up against first.

Ricky had deliberately lured Tetsuo to this spot.

A sigh of understanding worked its way out of my lungs. Tetsuo had never stood a chance. I had always thought the people who spent their time in Sanchōme were subpar players who used it as a glorified chat room. Clearly, I had some rethinking to do.

Tetsuo pushed open the doors of the saloon.

The walls were dressed in the same dim textures they had worn when I was last here. A man in a black tuxedo crouched in a seat at the bar. The heavyweight bartender from my previous visit was nowhere to be seen, and there was no one else in the saloon. Tetsuo and the man in the tuxedo were alone.

Tiny russet butterflies decorated his tie. He wore black leather shoes. A pair of purple cufflinks completed his outfit. I took him to be a lightweight jujutsuka.

One of us had to break the ice, so I pulled out my keyboard.

> Hi.
> Good day, Tetsuo.
> How do you know my name?

> We met at the wall dividing Itchōme and Sanchōme.

His facial texture looked familiar. This must have been the jujutsuka practicing E-rank jumps by the wall.

> Weren't you wearing a ninja outfit last time?
> I was scouting. Shinobi attire would be out of place in an establishment such as this.

He nodded his head knowingly, but his expression never changed. He seemed more a caricature of a ninja than anything, but I thought better of pointing that out. He continued.

> Alas, you are too early. Ricky never comes before eleven.
> I'm not here for a rematch.
> Is that so?

Tetsuo stood only three and a half steps from the ninja-cum-secret agent. Just out of dash-throw range. Dropping him into a battle stance, I shifted Tetsuo to the side, minimizing his exposed profile.

> Who told you my name? And how did you know I fought Ricky? I never told anyone in the saloon who I was.
> I made inquiries.
> With who?
> There is a certain individual who wears a button-down school uniform and high wooden clogs. I thought he might know who you were, so I went to the arena to ask. People seem to consider you a dark horse in the upcoming tournament, Tetsuo.
> Why go to all that trouble?
> I am ninja.
> That's not a reason.
> You may not consider it a reason, but alas, it is the only

one I have to offer. In this city, I am ninja. I collect meaningless information the way you engage in meaningless fights. A hobby of mine, nothing more.

> I never said it was meaningless.

> One man's meaning is another man's static.

> True enough.

I wanted to be the best player in the city. Hell, most people who played this game did. But this jujutsuka was different, and he knew it. While other characters were practicing their combos, he was searching for secret paths and paying visits to empty saloons.

The jujutsuka stood.

> Forgive me for not introducing myself sooner. I am Hashimoto, a collector of information.

Hashimoto bent at the waist in a graceful bow.

Leaping lightly over the counter, he took two beer bottles from the shelf behind the bar. He sent one bottle sliding across the bar toward Tetsuo.

> Won't we get in trouble?

> For what?

> I don't know, moving around his drinks. The heavyweight bartender won't get mad?

> Ben is not the bartender.

> He's not?

> This establishment belongs to no one. Ben only plays the role of bartender, as I am doing now. Role-playing, as it were.

The player controlling Hashimoto, a make-believe character who lived in a make-believe world, was suggesting that his character's goals and desires were somehow separate from his own. Somewhere in RL, someone was role-playing Hashimoto, a character who himself played the role of a ninja in Sanchōme. It was like opening a Russian matryoshka doll to find another doll nested inside. The only place you could do something like that was online.

Hashimoto tilted his head back and raised the beer to his mouth. Of course no liquid came spilling out of the polygonal bottle, and the texture on Hashimoto's face never changed. But I still found myself growing thirsty.

The JTS Saloon provided a refuge for characters who didn't fit in anywhere else in the game, characters who spent their time leaping over paper-thin walls and passing around polygonal glasses of beer.

> This place seems like a pretty well-kept secret. Why tell me how to get here?
> I was preoccupied with more…pressing concerns.
> Like what?
> My whisperers told me Jack might make an appearance. I was standing watch with my eagle eye.

The drunken fist in the skin-tight purple suit had said no one knew more about Jack than Hashimoto. Well, I had found him, and he had sent me on a wild goose chase to the JTS Saloon to learn more about Jack at the very moment he expected Jack to make an entrance.

> You lied to me.
> I misled you. There's a difference.
> You didn't think I had a chance against Jack, so you chased me off, is that it?

There was a long pause before he answered. When he finally did, a bubble filled almost to overflowing appeared over his head.

> Not at all. You appeared to be a skilled warrior. Had you

fought Jack, his health would have been diminished. You might even have slain him. But my objective is to discover Jack's true identity. Had you defeated him, it would have complicated things considerably.

> If he really wants to log out, all he has to do is pull out his LAN cable.

> Jack would never employ such measures. He has similar predilections to my own. When Jack defeats a foe, he always logs out using the proper mechanism. I have no doubt of this. It may be that, like me, he changes his textures each time he logs in.

When your health dropped to zero anywhere outside the arena, you were forced to log out. Since player information was kept private, once someone logged out, there was no way to find out who they were. Which is exactly why a roaming mystery ganker could exist in the first place. Unless a sysadmin performed an investigation, the ganker's identity would remain a mystery forever. But if there was a character role-playing Ganker Jack, as Hashimoto was suggesting, it would be possible to nail down the identity of the ordinary Versus Town citizen who was assuming Jack's identity at the character management system in Itchōme.

Hashimoto wanted to witness the moment Jack made the transformation back to average citizen for himself.

> Why tell me all this?

> You show great promise. I have heard there is no one in the arena who can defeat you. In time, Jack will surely seek you out.

> So I'm the sacrificial pig?

> I see no reason for you to disparage yourself so.

> I'd think someone like Ricky would be a better bet.

> I think not. Ricky finds fault with everyone who walks through those doors. He can make an excuse to fight anyone.

Only three people who frequent the saloon have beaten him.

> Who?

> Keith, 963, and Masumi.

> He beat Pak?

> Pak does not street fight. He declined Ricky's challenge.

That didn't change the fact that Ricky was damn good. Two of the three names Hashimoto listed were in the top four. He'd beaten just about everyone else.

> It is my opinion that you are slightly better than Ricky.

> But he beat me.

> Ricky held the terrain advantage. He was able to land a counterattack because of the hollow at the foot of the column. You are not the first to fall for this ploy. Sanchōme poses many challenges for the hardcore.

> You guys seem to have a specific meaning when you say *hardcore*.

> We use it to describe those who do naught but shut themselves away in the arena to fight.

> Then I guess I'm hardcore.

> So why come here at such a deserted hour?

For a moment, I imagined a twinkle in the eye of his immutable face.

> I needed to know how I'd been countered.

> The hollow by the column?

> That's the one.

Holding the beer bottle in one hand, Hashimoto leapt back over the counter. He landed on the polygonal floor with a flourish and extended his hand toward Tetsuo.

> Then next time, you will win.

~

For the next three days, Tetsuo explored Sanchōme in the hours I knew most others would be offline. I wanted to know every inch of Versus Town. I searched online for maps, but nothing I found had the level of detail I was looking for.

In a shooter, memorizing the location where each enemy appeared gave you an edge. In a strategy game, you needed to know what tactics to use for each map. Information was just as important in a fighting game. I had lost once because of a slight hollow in the ground, and I wasn't going to make the same mistake again.

Slipping between two nearly identical buildings, Tetsuo traced a gentle curve through the alleyways. At times he walked along the tops of walls, slipping and falling as he went. At others, he ran down the streets, leaping over polygonal obstacles barring his path. Tetsuo walked through Sanchōme block by block as I mapped the city on 5 mm graph paper. Compared to running, walking was painfully slow. You never seemed to get anywhere. But since I was marking down the location of every depression in the ground and every polygonal brick that had fallen out of a wall, running was not an option. Mapping Sanchōme was proving to be more difficult than a dungeon in a role-playing game.

Tetsuo passed through an alley no wider than his body and came face-to-face with a towering wall. The boundary separating Itchōme and Sanchōme was lined with E-rank walls like this one. There weren't meant to be shortcuts between the two areas, but by some happy accident someone had discovered that even these walls could be scaled.

The system wasn't designed to handle someone doing two air blocks at the apex of a high jump to shift their center of gravity to the other side of a wall. Most games contained exploits like this that the developers had never considered. E-rank wall jumping was one such exploit. The kind the players who gathered in the JTS Saloon knew inside and out.

Tetsuo ran along the base of the wall that divided the city. The unchanging sky spread overhead. Looking up, the scene reminded me of the narrow skies over Shinjuku.

Try though he might, Tetsuo couldn't make it over the wall. Heavyweight characters had a lot of power in their attacks at the price of mobility. Lightweight characters didn't deal much damage with each hit, but they were nimble and fast. Middleweights fell somewhere in between. It took a lightweight like Hashimoto to scale an E-rank wall.

For a character who could wall-jump, the JTS Saloon wasn't all that far from Itchōme, but a middleweight like Tetsuo had to take the long way round.

Tetsuo threaded his way back through a winding alley. It was almost eleven thirty at night. People would be filtering into Sanchōme soon. Tetsuo ran down a hidden alley he'd discovered earlier that day. He climbed a low wall and slipped between two houses, running straight across the yard of a Japanese-style home. He broke into a red-roofed Western home through a window and ran out the back door. This route shaved what would have been a fifteen-minute journey down to seven.

As Tetsuo darted out of an alley into a small adjoining square, two characters appeared at the edge of the screen. I pressed the A button to stop running. Tetsuo turned to face them.

One of the characters was a capoeirista in a chocolate-brown jacket that fit snugly about the waist. A camouflage texture covered his military-style pants. His lace-up boots and leather gloves were the same brown as his jacket. He was a heavyweight fighter with tousled blond hair.

The other character was a middleweight snake boxer. He wore a black tank top and black leather pants. A white skull was dyed into the texture on his back. A black wristband ringed his forearm. Where his eyes and mouth should have been he wore a sinister mask done up like the toothy designs the Americans painted on the noses of their bombers during the war.

The two fighters faced each other across an empty fountain in the middle of the square.

The masked snake boxer blurred into motion. Darting across the fountain he circled to the left of the capoeirista. The capoeirista responded with a middle forward kick. The snake boxer canceled out of his move and sprang back to his original position before retaliating with a low kick of his own. The capoeirista's health inched lower. He chased after the snake boxer with a speed dash. Breaking the capoeirista's dash with a crouching punch, the snake boxer back-dashed into the middle of the fountain.

Their fight raged through the slums of Sanchōme.

The capoeirista I had seen before. A blond-haired soldier in a leather jacket. I knew I was looking at Keith, one of the top four players in Versus Town. The masked snake boxer, however, was someone new. Whoever he was, he was matching one of the top four step for step, blow for blow. Maybe even *out*matching him.

Keith placed one foot inside the fountain. The masked man threw his fastest punch. Keith blocked. The masked man closed the distance, chaining another attack seamlessly onto the punch he'd just thrown. Keith inched backwards, artfully avoiding each attack.

Keith launched a middle spin kick in the hair of a pause between two of his opponent's attacks. The masked man dodged with a crouching back dash, moving toward the center of the fountain. Keith canceled out of the spin kick and did a speed dash. The masked man kept moving. Keith's foot came to rest on the rim of the fountain.

It was just like the fight between Tetsuo and Ricky. While the masked man crouched inside the fountain, any attacks Keith made from the fountain's edge would sail harmlessly over his head.

But Keith didn't attack.

Adjusting his angle, Keith speed-dashed to the side of the

masked man, drawing up beside him. They were so close their polygons were overlapping. Keith did a handstand, catching his opponent's neck between his legs.

The two fighters collapsed in a tangle of arms and legs, separating in the middle of the fountain. Keith back-dashed. Once more the fountain stood between them.

Keith hadn't made the same mistake Tetsuo did. The move that had caught the masked man's neck between his legs was a capoeira throw. Keith had recognized there was a danger his attacks could miss and switched up. Unfortunately for Keith, the masked man had responded with a throw break. He had managed to get off the one command that could save him and had done it with only milliseconds to act.

The masked man circled the fountain. Keith advanced to head him off from the right, striking with a middle kick. The masked man backed away to the left, stepping out of the incoming kick. Keith followed hard with another kick. To keep things interesting, he threw in a cancel move, forcing the masked man back step by step to avoid the barrage of blows.

A brick-textured wall pressed close behind the masked man's back. A white windowsill jutted from the wall's face. A polygonal potted plant was visible through the glass. Just as fighting from the low ground put you at a disadvantage, having your back up against a wall didn't do you any favors either. If you took a hit, your body made a good target for midair combos as it rebounded off the wall.

Keith had backed the masked man into a corner. He threw a crouching punch, but the masked man blocked. Keith chained a low kick onto the punch, but the masked man hopped above the sweep of his leg. Keith canceled out of the low kick and into a rising toe kick. Still hanging in the air, there was no way the masked man could dodge. The kick connected.

The counterhit sound FX played and the masked man soared through the air. As his body rebounded off the wall, he did an air block. Moving forward, Keith threw his fastest punch.

The masked man did another air block as Keith punched. His center of gravity shifted and his body caught on the white windowsill. Keith's punch missed.

Using the wall as a springboard, the masked man jumped down and landed behind Keith, still off-balance from his attack moments before. The masked man spun around and struck Keith in the back with an open-palmed thrust. The counterhit sound FX played again.

Now Keith's body rose into the air. The masked man threw a punch, canceled, and punched again. Keith's body crashed into the wall. The masked man caught Keith's rebounding body with another open-palmed thrust and speed-dashed forward. Canceling out of the dash he punched again. And again. He finished the attack with a reverse roundhouse kick. Keith's lifeless body grated against the wall, sliding slowly to the ground.

Keith vanished from the screen.

The entire fight had lasted only a few seconds.

Tetsuo immediately walked toward the masked man.

> Hey.

The masked man wheeled around. He stood 45 degrees to Tetsuo's right, exactly three and a half steps away. Just outside of dash-throw range. Words bubbled over his head.

> Enjoy the show?
> Who are you?
> See you around.

The masked man broke into a run.

I pulled my hands away from the keyboard and grabbed the controls, jabbing the stick twice to the right. Tetsuo took off in pursuit. They were both middleweight characters, so they ran at the same speed.

The masked man ducked into an alley. It was a virtual

obstacle course. The ceiling was too low to stand and walk, so he wave-dashed through with a string of crouch dashes. Outside again, he bolted across the yard of a large house and turned a corner, his speed never dropping below a flat-out run.

Little by little, he pulled away from Tetsuo. The way he moved, I could tell he knew the placement of every brick in every building. If I hadn't just been out mapping Sanchōme, I would have lost him completely in less than ten seconds.

Suddenly the man burst out into the middle of a wide empty square. Ahead, the wall dividing Itchōme and Sanchōme towered above us. Tall buildings hemmed us in on either side. Above the wall, two butter roll clouds drifted against a perfect turquoise blue sky.

Tetsuo followed the masked man into the dead end. The man turned around slowly. A middleweight couldn't jump an E-rank wall.

Out of nowhere, the masked man turned and did a round-house kick. A loud *clang* sound FX reverberated. His kick had hit a metal drum. If he'd meant to hit Tetsuo, he wasn't even close. The drum rolled off with a deep bass rumble.

I pulled out my keyboard, typing as fast as I could. A bubble appeared over Tetsuo's head.

> You're him, aren't you??

The man chased after the metal drum. He caught up with it three steps from the wall and hopped on top. Using the drum as a stepping-stone, he leaped into the air. He gave the command for an air block, and at the apex of his jump his body twisted to the side. The polygons of his body caught on the top of the wall. He did another air block. His center of gravity shifted, and he disappeared as he slid down the far side of the wall.

With seeming ease, the masked snake boxer had scaled a wall I thought impossible for any middleweight character. He had gotten away.

The E-rank wall towered over Tetsuo. He was alone in the slums of Sanchōme.

I had seen Keith, one of the top four, fall before my eyes. He was an excellent player, worthy of the reputation he had earned for himself. But the masked man was even better. He had handled each of Keith's attacks with cold precision, and his ploy—deliberately allowing himself to be hit in order to lull his opponent into a false sense of security—was exquisite.

Exhausted, I stared at the screen.

~

The street fight, the chase through Sanchōme. There wasn't any doubt. I had finally found Ganker Jack.

Tonight's score: 0 wins, 0 losses.

CHAPTER 8

A LISTLESS BREEZE BLEW THROUGH SHINJUKU over the sickening heat of sunlit asphalt. Tall buildings walled in the city like the sides of some giant wine bottle. The thick air was the cloudy dregs of the wine clinging to the back of my neck.

I walked along Ome Highway toward school. It was 9:42 AM. I checked the bulletin board before heading to my logic class. In the room, I threaded my way between the downturned heads of students diligently taking notes and sat down in the dim seat by the wall, seven rows from the front.

"You're late." Fumiko cast a withering glance in my direction from the corner of her eye.

"Sorry." I fought back a yawn. "What color today?"

"Orange. You're really slacking off, you know that?" she added before melting back into the note-scribbling masses.

Another yawn rose in my throat, but with Herculean effort, I suppressed it. I hadn't gotten nearly enough sleep over the past few days. I rested my cheek on the cool desktop.

The sound FX of a dawn redwood rustling in the wind.

The sound FX of a truck trundling along Ome Highway.

The sound FX of Fumiko's eraser attacking her paper.

The world was filled with sound FX. But just then, I didn't have the energy to care. Even without earbuds, the noise washing over me remained distant.

I took an orange attendance card out of my pencil case and shut my eyes.

"You feeling okay?"

My eyes opened at the sound of Fumiko's voice. "Yeah, I'm fine."

"You were out cold."

I lifted my head and looked around the room. The only people left were a handful of chatting students, Fumiko, and me. Of Uemura the Elder, there was no sign. The sea of gently bobbing heads had vanished without a trace.

"Did the bell ring?"

"About ten minutes ago."

"I must not have heard it."

"Obviously."

"But I always hear it..." I rubbed my eyes. No matter how tired I was, I always woke at the first chirp from my digital clock. The sound of my dad flushing the toilet in the morning would wake me up. I had to close the shutters on my window to keep out the noise from the busy street in front of our house, or that would wake me up too.

"You've been playing that game again."

"Yeah."

"I don't see what's so fun about it." There was something peculiar in her voice.

I ran my fingers through my hair. It was still warm from the nap. "It's not about having fun."

"Then what is it about?"

"Blocking out the noise."

"That again." She raised her eyebrows and let out a long, deep sigh. "Better hurry or we'll be late for the next class."

Fumiko dragged me by the bag strap to our political economy class. The air in the halls was cool. Sunlight bathed the campus. We sat in the same seats we always did, seven rows from the front. The familiar bell sound FX signaled the start of class, and Fumiko took her glasses out of their plastic case with Pavlovian timing. I was drifting, only halfway in the real world. There was a haze in my head that wouldn't clear.

~

The next day I managed a little time for myself between

classes, so I went out into Shinjuku. For most people, Shinjuku was a place they came to accomplish some particular task. Some came in search of material things, or entertainment, or pleasure, and others came to provide them. The pimps and recruiters looking for girls to star in cheap adult videos were always busy. The only people without anything to do were college students like me and Fumiko, and the homeless.

Fumiko would probably get upset at being grouped with me. After all, she had her blue cat of happiness to look for.

From the outside looking in, I didn't have the vaguest notion whether she was shopping or looking for that cat. Like most women, she preferred being in nice, pretty places. If the cat she was looking for really was a ghost, it seemed unlikely to turn up in the accessories department of the Takashimaya Times Square department store, but she insisted otherwise. She gave the homeless man outside a wide berth. He was standing by the entrance to one of the many tunnels that crisscrossed beneath the city streets. Admittedly, by June most homeless gave off a fairly aromatic bouquet. Harmless as they were, I could hardly blame Fumiko for wanting to avoid them, but if you asked me where I thought we were more likely to turn up leads on the cat, the squalid back streets seemed more promising.

People who lived in RL didn't stand around waiting to spill their innermost secrets to you the moment you walked up, so I was only marking off the areas—not the people—on my map as "checked." As I ticked off one graph paper box after another, it occurred to me that the heroes in all those role-playing games must be extremely sociable. The emphasis of the games was always on the challenge of vanquishing some great evil, but maybe what really made a hero was his uncanny ability to glean information from the local villagers. The villagers in RL tended to scurry off to their jobs and whatnot without a word. Not that I was much of a hero. I was probably closer to being an NPC—call me Villager A.

That day I spied a villager in front of the arcade near Shinjuku

Koma Theater who looked as though she might have some morsel of information. She wasn't made-up. Her reddish brown hair was disheveled. The shawl—or was it a cloak?—draped over her shoulders streamed lazily behind her in the damp air. The bat lady. She was buying canned coffee from a vending machine. Two cans.

Passing through the sliding glass doors, I followed her into the arcade. As I walked inside, a slightly cooler but still humid mass of air poured over me, its fragrance a blend of molding carpet, plastic rubbed smooth, and rusted coins. Removing my earbuds, I moved deeper into the arcade. A tsunami of game music and sound FX so violent I could almost see the sound waves crashed over my body and broke against my eardrums.

Several patrons were already inside. One sat at a strip mahjong game. Win a game and you got to see a famous porn star in all her glory. Another sat at an electronic card game examining a hand of digital cards. Both were dressed in suit and tie. The man playing the card game had tossed his bright red tie over his shoulder and was staring intently at the screen. From time to time he would mop sweat from his brow with a handkerchief, check the cards in his digital hand, and then mop his brow again.

The bat lady wasn't playing games. She was sitting with her legs crossed beside a machine at the back of the arcade. The same machine that had gotten me into a back alley fight with a couple of guys I'd never seen before in my life because Fumiko wanted revenge. It was the latest iteration of the *Versus Town* arcade game.

Someone else was playing the game. I passed behind the man playing the card game and looked at the screen out of the corner of my eye. He wasn't very good, and that was putting it nicely. To put it less nicely, watching him maneuver was the visual equivalent of fingernails on a chalkboard.

A row of hundred-yen coins sat lined up on the face of the

machine. The guy was getting a new GAME OVER screen every minute or two, but it didn't stop him from dropping in the next coin and trying again. The bat lady didn't seem to be in a hurry to take over for him.

She noticed me and waved me over. I walked closer.

The man sitting at the machine was old. His gray hairs far outnumbered the black. He was neatly dressed and groomed, and he didn't look like someone who would be in an arcade at this hour—or any hour—of the day. He spoke above the din.

"Hey, Lui."

"Yes, sir?"

"I pushed the red button, but he didn't punch."

"You have to push the green button first. You want to press the green button once, then the red one twice, and then the blue one twice."

"I thought the green button was for blocking."

"That's right, but you also use it to cancel a move you already started. Since you buffered a throw break on the back of your last attack, you needed to cancel everything to clear your commands and start over." She knew her stuff, but it was all going right over the old man's head. "Here, let me show you."

The bat lady the old man had called Lui took his place at the controls. An eagle claw appeared in the middle of the screen. When the computer-controlled character attacked, Lui pressed the green button once, the red button twice, and then the blue button twice. Her hands moved quickly, but not so much that it was unclear what she was doing. Had she input the commands any slower, the combo wouldn't have registered. The move was exquisitely timed. The old man gave an involuntary cry of admiration.

Her style of play seemed strangely familiar.

Girl gamers were a rare breed. The vast majority of us were guys. This was especially true in *Versus Town*, a game which was very unforgiving. There were plenty of female characters, sure, but 99 percent of them were being played by men. They didn't do it to pretend to be women; it was nothing that Freudian. It was a question of what you preferred staring at all day. Besides, even if they looked like women, the moment they opened their mouths they wouldn't be fooling anybody.

Bedlam erupted whenever people found out that a female character was actually being played by a girl. There were always one or two players too socially challenged to handle direct contact with members of the opposite sex, and the others would have to step in and throw virtual buckets of cold water on them. It wasn't that the men who played online games formed some sort of anti-stalker brigade, but when the male to female ratio was that out of whack to begin with, special measures to maintain the social order rose of their own accord. Women like Lui who played online games often pretended to be men to avoid the whole issue.

The old man had taken up the controls again. I spoke to Lui in a low voice.

"What's going on? Why did you call him 'sir'?"

"He's the president of a big company. Or used to be, anyway. He's one of our regulars. Started coming by about two years ago. The only thing he can get his grandson to do with him is play video games."

"You play *VT*." It wasn't a question.

There was a long pause before she said, "Alas, I am sworn to secrecy." She winked at me. Not a lot of people talked like that, but I could think of one person who did.

"You gotta be kidding."

Lui shrugged indifferently. I started to ask her another question, but she raised her index finger and pressed it gently against her lips. "Best not to mix realities. What's real is real. What's not is not. Right?"

The old man finished playing. He was breathing so hard you'd have thought he'd just run a marathon. "I don't understand," he panted. "What do kids see in these games?"

"It's a place where they can rebel, sir. A place where they're not separated into adults and children, rich and poor. You must remember what that was like."

"A video game rebellion," he muttered to himself.

"Social revolution, the internal violence of the student movement," Lui said. "When you get down to it, they didn't result in any real change. It's all make-believe. But finding people you can share a common language with? That's real."

"Hmm. Never thought of it that way." There was a hint of awe in his voice.

Staring into the screen, his eyes transformed from those of an old toothless dog into a bird of prey. The game he'd seen as nothing more than a way of getting his grandson's attention had suddenly taken on a new meaning, one to which he could relate. He removed his bifocals from his breast pocket and leaned in to read the basic moves written on the control panel with newfound enthusiasm.

I leaned over to Lui and whispered, "Rebellion? Social revolution?"

"I was interpreting. All the explanations in the world won't do any good if he doesn't understand them."

"Wow. I'm impressed."

"It's something you learn to do in my line of work. You have to be able to talk your way into someone's trust when you're making a pitch." Her voice rang with pride. "Not the sort of thing you learn from a textbook."

I stared at her. Whatever preconceptions I might have had of the type of woman who would accompany an old man to an arcade in the middle of the day so he could learn to play video games with his grandson, she didn't fit them.

She feigned offense. "Was it something I said?"

"Not really."

"You look upset."

"I've never been good at talking people into things."

"No one said anything about talking them into things they don't *want*." She puffed out her cheeks. She was still just young enough to pull the look off. Not that I knew how old she was, but if I had to guess, I'd say she was somewhere between two and five years older than me.

"So what is it then?" I asked.

"Think of it as…role-playing."

"Not that again."

"What do you mean?"

"The other day you told me Ganker Jack was only role-playing." I frowned. "Or, let me guess. That wasn't you, that was Hashimoto, and you've got your own take on the whole thing."

Lui gave a vague nod that could have meant anything. The only thing that was clear was that she didn't want to expand on our virtual conversation here in RL.

The old man's eyes were still riveted to the control panel. He spoke without looking up. "That your new boyfriend?"

"If he buys me a condo I might consider it," Lui answered through pale, naked lips.

"It's always about the money with you."

"Your grandson's the one you should be worried about. Before you know it he'll be begging you for a Porsche or BMW, not coins for arcade games."

"A Mercedes, now *that's* a car."

When we met in the virtual world, I thought Hashimoto was a bit weird. But now I realized we actually had a lot in common. Maybe Lui, who role-played in RL as much as in virtual life, saw the world through the same veil I did. Maybe she heard the same sound FX.

It reminded me of a girlfriend I'd had in high school. She had straight brown hair that streamed behind her when she walked. She was beautiful; a person of few words like myself. I think people wondered how two people who talked so little were able to communicate, but we always understood each other. I realized if I'd been born a woman, I would have been just like her.

Correction.

Had I been born a woman, I wouldn't have had half so pretty a face.

~

The next time I saw the bat lady was in Kabuki-chō Nichōme.

As usual, Fumiko was in class, and as usual, I had time to kill. I walked the alleys with blue-cat-hunting highlighter and map in hand.

Nichōme was famous for its gay community. There was a sushi bar there—the entire restaurant consisted of a counter with a well-muscled sushi chef behind it—that everyone at our school called Bert's because the man behind the counter had a caterpillar-like eyebrow that made him look like the character from *Sesame Street*. I still don't know what the real name of the place was.

I doubt it had anything to do with Nichōme in particular, but walking by myself I started to understand Fumiko's irrational fear of the homeless lurking under the eaves of the buildings. So when I heard someone shout out my name from behind me, I let out an uncharacteristic yelp.

"Didn't mean to scare you." The bat lady's trademark cloak-or-was-it-a-shawl hung from her shoulders. She gave me a bracing pat on the back hard enough to send me into a small coughing fit. The cat map caught Lui's eye. "What's that?"

"A map."

"Running errands for someone?"

"Actually, yes. I'm looking for the blue cat."

Lui took the map from my hand. "I've never seen anyone taking the search so seriously. You writing a book or something?"

"If you want to find a rare item in a game, you either use a strategy guide or make your own map. I haven't seen any blue cat strategy guides lately." I held out my hand. "I'll take that back now."

"Good luck making it work in RL."

"It works in games. Why not here?"

"How do you know where one square ends and the next begins?"

"I manage."

I had to admit, it hadn't been easy marking off the places we'd already looked. But compared to mapping every pothole in Versus Town, looking for clues to the whereabouts of the blue cat was a piece of cake. RL might have contained a nearly infinite amount of data, but there was nothing that said we needed to put it all down on the map. Anything that didn't pertain to the search was just noise.

My cell phone rang in my pocket. It was Fumiko. Class had been canceled at the last minute, so she wanted to join the search party. She was already in Kabuki-chō, about thirty meters from where I was standing. I had told her I planned to map the area near Bert's today.

Fumiko appeared from around the corner. She looked surprised to see me standing next to the bat lady.

"This your girlfriend?" Lui nudged me with her elbow.

I snatched the cat map from her hand. A sidelong glance at Fumiko revealed a complicated expression on her face, no doubt laden with subtle and profound meaning that I was having trouble reading in my current flustered state. Had her hamburger-shop smile greeted me, I would have answered yes without hesitation. Unfortunately, Fumiko's message was somewhat less clear. I stalled for time with a noncommittal smile.

"Who's this?" Fumiko's turn to interrogate.

As an answer coalesced in my head, I realized there wasn't much information I knew about Lui that I would feel comfortable sharing in front of her. I suspected she worked in a nightclub of some sort, but I wasn't sure. The only reason I even knew her name was that I'd overheard an old man call her that in an arcade. I knew more about her alternate persona, a ninja named Hashimoto who searched a virtual city night after night for a virtual person known as Ganker Jack. Any way you looked at it, the answer would have come off sounding crazy.

Lui produced a slender cigarette from the folds of her clothes and lit it. "I'm Shinjuku Townsperson A."

Fumiko's eyebrows shot upward. "What kind of answer is that?"

"She's all right. I run into her around here sometimes. I was asking her about the blue cat."

"That's right," answered Lui, taking a slow drag from her cigarette. Tendrils of white smoke twisted and swirled as they dispersed in the sky above the alley. Lui clapped me on the back with a cloth-draped arm that resembled a bat wing. "Don't wander around here with a sweet thing like that too long. Your wolfish instincts might get the better of you."

"Don't worry, I'm not cool enough to be a wolf. Not until I get some payback for that fight, at least. Until then, I'm just another pig to the slaughter."

"*Resurrection of Golden Wolf*," interjected Fumiko.

"What's that?" I asked.

"It's a famous movie. That was the tagline. 'The wolf lives, and the pigs go to slaughter.'"

"You're just full of trivia."

"It's an old movie anyway."

"I prefer sheep," chimed Lui. "There has to be more to the world than wolves and pigs. Sheep might not be the smartest animals, but I'll take them over wolves and pigs any day."

"So you're more *Silence of the Lambs*."

"A movie buff, are you?"

"What if I am?"

"Nothing. I happen to like Anthony Hopkins."

They were speaking a code I didn't understand. "Let's go."

I gave Lui a nod as she took another pull on her cigarette. Fumiko had already started walking off. She disappeared around the corner of a narrow alley. I looked back and forth between Lui and the street Fumiko had turned down.

"Go on, chase after her."
Cat map in hand, I did just that.

CHAPTER 9

> HEY, KARATEKA. YOU TETSUO?
Text bubbled over the man's head.
> That's me.
> Let's fight.

It had been less than forty seconds since I'd logged in to *Versus Town*. The man called out to Tetsuo as he ran down Main Street, the broad thoroughfare leading out of Itchōme. Dirt and stain textures covered his martial arts uniform. He wore a black wristband. His feet were bare. A large toothpick protruded from the corner of the mouth texture on his face. He looked like a heavyweight drunken fist.

Without another word, he attacked. I crouched to duck under his leading punch and backed Tetsuo off to the right.

> You running?

Keeping one hand on the stick, I tapped out a reply on the keyboard.

> No, but you'll wish I had.

Drunken fist is a Chinese martial art so named because its techniques resemble the erratic stagger of a drunk. The unpredictable and unusual moves are meant to confuse the opponent. It's a fun school to play and watch, but it's not very effective in a streetfight. It was unusual to see a drunken fist rise to the rank of black wrist street fighter.

I counted slowly to three before giving the speed dash

command. Tetsuo rushed forward.

The drunken fist stumbled back to the right as he swung at Tetsuo with a backhand. Tetsuo pivoted to the left out of the way of the oncoming attack and launched a middle kick. The drunken fist blocked. Tetsuo threw his fastest punch, then immediately canceled out of the move and executed a dash-throw combo. He grabbed the drunken fist by the back of the neck and head-butted him, sending him sprawling onto the ground.

I spied a lamppost at the edge of the screen. Tetsuo circled the post in a broad arc. The drunken fist rose and followed. Exchanging minor blows with his opponent, Tetsuo retreated. A wall textured with concrete blocks loomed at his back.

When there was no more room to back up, the drunken fist charged. I was ready for him. I pressed the stick up and to the right. Tetsuo jumped toward the lamppost. Just before hitting the post Tetsuo air-blocked, then pushed off the post to land behind the drunken fist. The drunken fist was still recovering from his last attack. Tetsuo finished him with a midair combo off a flying knee kick.

The turquoise blue sky stretched overhead. A motley selection of characters ran along the right side of Main Street. Unchanging shadows stretched across the gray-textured ground.

It was 11:30 PM.

> Another one bites the dust.

I meant to say it to myself, but I typed it without even realizing. Cursing under my breath, I grabbed hold of the stick. Tetsuo turned down an alley off Main Street and started making his way toward Sanchōme.

Ever since Ganker Jack had shown up, street fights had become increasingly common. The white headband Tetsuo wore signaled that he belonged to the most skilled group of street fighters. It also meant he was honor-bound to accept any and all challenges. When a worthy opponent presented himself, Tetsuo was happy to fight. In Versus Town, fights made the world go round.

But in the last week, things had gotten out of hand. The drunken fist I'd just wiped the floor with wasn't the worst player in the game, but he was a few miles short of the best. He was only slightly better than the average player Tetsuo faced in the arena. If he really wanted to improve, he needed to put in some serious arena time practicing combos before he started wandering the streets picking fights.

Then there was the fact that the drunken fist had addressed Tetsuo by name. He had known Tetsuo would be coming, and he'd been waiting for him on Main Street. That was something else entirely.

Hashimoto was using Tetsuo as bait. He had started a rumor in the arena about a karateka named Tetsuo, and now he was waiting for Jack to move in for the kill. Hashimoto knew the route Tetsuo took from Itchōme to the JTS Saloon. He had lookouts tucked in every corner of Versus Town just waiting for Ganker Jack to show his stripes. In the meantime, every fighter in the city looking to make a name for himself was hunting Tetsuo as if he had a bright red target on his chest.

Watching Hashimoto go happily about his search for Jack's true identity, I wondered whether it was the prospect of finding out the truth that kept him going or simply the joy of the hunt. I had promised Hashimoto I would help, so I could hardly complain. And besides, I had to tip my hat to him for even making the attempt. But for Hashimoto to learn Jack's identity, Tetsuo had to lose to him. That was the rub. Hashimoto didn't think Tetsuo could beat Jack. It was a weird sort of expectation to try to live up to.

Tetsuo pushed through the double swinging doors of the JTS Saloon and stepped inside.

> Mineral water, my good man.
> Comin' right up.

The glass came sliding at Tetsuo across the bar. He caught it in his right hand without missing a beat and moved toward the back of the saloon. Tetsuo picked his way between decrepit chairs, heading for the darkest spot in a dark room. He found Hashimoto there, sitting quietly at a round table.

> Hey.
> Once again we come up…empty-handed.
> Looks like.

Tetsuo caught the leg of a nearby chair with a middle round-house and sat down before continuing the conversation.

> These past three days I've started wishing the skeptics were right about Jack.
> You know better. You saw him with your own two eyes.
> I'm just starting to feel the downside of being a black wrist.
> We each have our cross to bear, whatever path we choose to walk.
> You always were a philosopher.
> I am ninja.
> Where's Masumi at, anyway?
> She hasn't arrived yet.
> It's not like her to get here after me.
> Indeed.

Tetsuo and Hashimoto continued chatting about nothing. Hashimoto was a creature of the virtual world. The comings and goings in Shinjuku, a place that existed in RL, meant nothing to him. When I tried steering the conversation in that direction, I was met with a wall of silence as indifferent and unchanging as the textures on his face.

It wasn't long before a drunken fist in a skin-tight purple suit walked through the doors. Masumi grabbed a glass off the counter without missing a step and headed toward the back of the saloon, just as Tetsuo had done a few minutes earlier.

Hooking a chair with a middle roundhouse, she joined us at the table. Text bubbled overhead.

> You're not gonna believe this.
> I've heard no whispers. What happened?
> He's too good. Inhuman.
> You fought Jack.
> Fought and lost. Not just lost, wtfpwned lost.

The best drunken fist in Versus Town crossed her legs. Masumi had finished second place in the first season tournament. She'd entered her eagle claw character in the tournament, but she'd since grown disenchanted with fighting and switched to her current character. Now she was living out a self-proclaimed retirement in this saloon in Sanchōme. She hadn't even signed up for the next tournament.

Compared to eagle claw, drunken fist was a weak school. In spite of that, Masumi could still go toe to toe with any of the top four. Text bubbled over her head again.

> None of my throws would connect.
> None of them?
> He throw-breaked every last one. One hundred percent.
> That's impossible.
> It is a...difficult account to believe.
> Well it's true. I wouldn't joke about something like this.
> How did he break your throws?

Masumi had elevated throws to an art form. She specialized in baited throws, waiting for her opponent to throw a punch in an effort to hold her at bay and then stepping up for the throw as he retracted his arm.

It was technically possible to avoid a throw using a throw break, but Masumi positioned herself just a few pixels out of range when waiting for her moment. She was already so close she didn't even need to speed-dash. There simply wasn't enough time to throw-break.

Tetsuo had sparred with her once. She had thrown him five times out of five attempts. It was a street fight, so she stopped before his health went to zero, but if the fight had been real, there was no doubt Tetsuo would have lost badly.

> He must have read the opening throw animation.
> No way, Masumi.
> Well, I can't think of what else it could be.
> Not even the computer could react at such speeds.
> It wasn't a computer. I know it wasn't.

The servers at Versus Town Networks, Inc., performed batch calculations on the polygons in the city. When a player input a command, it was converted to a signal that traveled through the network. After the game servers processed the command, they sent back information about the polygons that needed to be displayed on-screen. The only thing the game consoles sitting in every player's home actually did was process the signals traveling in and out of the house and render the graphics onto the screen.

It took one-fifteenth of a second from the time a player input a command to the time the effects of that command could be seen on the screen. A throw break would only register in the quarter of a second immediately following a successful throw. If what Masumi said was true, Jack had split the difference. He had seen her throw coming and given the throw-break command in the smallest fraction of a second.

It didn't sit right with me.

> I don't think a human can react that fast.
> I've seen people press a button sixteen times a second. Who's to say someone couldn't read a throw coming that fast?
> Button-mashing and split-second decision-making are

two different things.

> There are those who can reverse a slide kick with a dragon punch.

> Wrong game.

> I even tried a trick throw at the end.

> Not a tactic you would usually employ. You have always shunned the Dark Arts.

> I had to see how good he was. But even that didn't work.

> That's crazy.

> I wanted to get near one of Hashimoto's lookouts, but he caught me in front of an E-rank wall. I never thought he'd attack in Itchōme.

> He outsmarted us.

> Even if I'd been on my eagle claw, I don't know if I could have beaten him. When I first heard he beat Keith, I didn't believe it. I do now.

Keith was as good as his reputation. But when I saw him face Jack in Sanchōme, it wasn't even a contest. Jack was in a whole other league from the top four. To hear Masumi tell it, he was even better than that.

Maybe Hashimoto was right. If Tetsuo fought Jack, Tetsuo might lose. Pak too for that matter. Somewhere in the twisting alleys of Sanchōme, Jack was stalking his prey.

> What sort of man is he?

Hashimoto wouldn't let any crumb of information fall through the cracks.

> I'd say he has a flair for the dramatic.

> How so?

> He asked why I changed to a drunken fist.

> And how did you respond?

> I told him I got tired of fighting in the arena, so I decided

to hang out in Sanchōme instead. He said that made me the
perfect enemy.
> What's that supposed to mean?
> Who knows? That's all he said.
> It would seem Jack has a philosophy of his own.
> You call that a philosophy?
> Ninja do not speak lies.

Hashimoto nodded sagely. Text appeared above Masumi's
head.

> Oh, I almost forgot. You made it through the first
round, Tetsuo. You and the top four were the only ones to go
undefeated.
> Whaddaya know.

The second season tournament was broken up into three
rounds: two preliminary elimination rounds and the final tournament. In the first round, eight hundred plus characters faced
each other in a handful of random matches, and the characters
with the best records advanced to the second round. Only the
top sixty made it. The second round would be tournament-style,
with the top fifteen characters advancing to the finals. As the
winner of the last tournament, Pak automatically qualified
for the finals without participating in the preliminary rounds.
Tetsuo had made it over the first hurdle.

Of the patrons of the JTS Saloon, only Ricky, Tetsuo, and
three of the top four had entered the tournament. Masumi and
the rest didn't seem to care.

Even though most of the JTS regulars were skilled players
who would win nine fights out of ten against lesser competitors,
fighting didn't interest them. They were content to gather in the
saloon each night and pass the time with meaningless chatter.
If they had entered the tournament, Tetsuo would rather face
one of the so-called hardcore over the JTS crowd any day.

> Indeed. Congratulations.
> Thanks.
> One other thing.

Masumi shrugged—her signature move.

>Your first match is against Ricky.

The controller slipped out of my hand. Tetsuo lost his balance
and tumbled out of the chair. I shouted a string of expletives
at the screen.

~

The arena was spacious and vast.

Compared to the intricate meshes that formed the mean-
dering streets of Sanchōme, the polygons in the arena were
gigantic. The walls were covered with bright-colored textures
that seemed oddly out of place. The only sound FX to be heard
were punches, kicks, and counterhits. Absent were the low
rumbles of rolling metal drums, the squeak from the hinges of
wooden doors, the warble of glass sliding across a bar.

It was ten minutes before Tetsuo's match with Ricky.

All of the matches in the tournament were one-game affairs.
There was a time limit for the two preliminary rounds, but none
for the finals. If you fell behind early in a preliminary match, it
would be hard to come back. You could lose by stepping out of
the ring, and there were no bumps or hollows in the ground.
Otherwise, it was just like fighting anywhere else.

Keeping the action of the second round at the edge of the
screen, I maneuvered Tetsuo around the periphery of the arena.
I had made the circuit one and a half times when I spotted
Ricky practicing on one of the training dummies. Tetsuo walked
over to him.

> Hey.

Ricky remained facing the dummy while text bubbled over his head.

> What do you want?
> Nothing, really.
> You getting butterflies?
> A little.
> That doesn't sound like you.
> Maybe not.
> Can't say I blame you. I feel another perfect victory coming.

Ricky turned his head. His face was a mask, frozen forever in a faint smile. Even so, he looked nervous.

> There aren't enough sounds here.
> What are you talking about?
> The sound FX all sound the same. It's so flat.
> It's the arena, what do you expect?
> Yeah, you're right.
> Look, you're a black wrist. You got that white headband on. The only reason to talk in the arena is to ask someone to fight. You should know that.
> Yeah.
> That's all I got to say then. We're gonna fight, and I'm gonna win again.
> Funny, I had the same idea. I just wanted to tell you something before the match.
> Spit it out.
> When we met, you said I wasn't a wolf, I was a pig to the slaughter.
> Yeah, so? If you think I'm gonna take it back, think again.

> The way I see it, there are more than just wolves and pigs. The world's not that simple. You and I aren't wolves. No one in Versus Town is. Or if they are, it's only because they role-play being wolves.

> What are you talking about?

My conversation with Lui had gotten me thinking. None of us was born to be a pig. We didn't lead sheltered lives with nothing to do but gorge ourselves and grow fat. If anything, we were wayward sheep. Someday we would grow quiet, and when that time came we would bungee jump into a wilderness seething with wolves. For some, the cord might snap, leaving them to struggle on broken limbs as the wolves descended to feed. Others might find a way to survive in the wilderness, shedding their snow white wool to live as wolves. The next sheep to come bungee jumping in would be their first meal.

Most of the sheep would scurry back home with only fleeting memories of something dark and evil to commemorate their ordeal. Safe within their pens, they could dream of the world of adventure they had glimpsed.

I was less than successful in conveying all of that to Ricky.

> You're messing up my timing. Leave me alone.
> Sorry, didn't mean to bother you.
> I beat you once, I can beat you again.
> I haven't forgotten. I'll never forget.

He had beaten me. Ricky was better than Tetsuo then.

No matter how good Tetsuo became, he could never erase that defeat. Like a world champion boxer who had lost a fight to the local bully when he was a kid. A defeat that would echo across the ages. Years later, sitting in a dingy bar, the middle-aged bully could boast that he beat the champ, and it would be true. It was better to accept a hard fact than struggle against it.

When Ricky beat Tetsuo, his corpse had sunk into a digital sea. I rode on the surface of that sea. The sea was my past. It had carried me where I was today.

Tetsuo moved away from Ricky. Ricky went back to practicing combos. Punch and kick sound FX reverberated. In those last minutes before the match, I left Tetsuo behind and became Etsuro Sakagami. I read a manga.

Then I pressed the A button and I was Tetsuo again. The first match of the second elimination round began. It was only the second time Tetsuo and Ricky had fought. Ricky never did street fight rematches.

Ricky back-dashed as soon as the match started. Just what I wanted to see. Tetsuo rushed forward, closing the gap between them. Still in a speed dash, Tetsuo threw a middle punch. I hadn't noticed that Ricky had already canceled out of the back dash. Ricky's response to Tetsuo's careless attack was immediate. He transitioned seamlessly from a crouching back dash to a headlong charge, delivering a brutal open-palmed thrust. A counterhit. Tetsuo's body lifted off the ground.

Ricky punched Tetsuo's airborne body once. Twice. He canceled into an elbow strike, then did a crouching punch. Tetsuo hit the ground. Ricky backed away without pressing the attack.

Tetsuo's health gauge had taken a big hit. He rose to his feet.

I wasn't thinking straight. I'd come into the fight expecting Ricky to back up right from the start. Ricky must have guessed as much, and he used it against me, just as he'd used that hollow at the base of the column outside JTS. He was good, no question about it.

Tetsuo moved forward and to the right. Ricky faked a forward charge, then canceled and moved off at an angle from Tetsuo. The two characters rotated 60 degrees counterclockwise around the center of the ring. Tetsuo threw his fastest punch. Ricky dodged with a crouching back dash. Tetsuo speed-dashed forward. He canceled out of a buffered punch and speed-dashed again. Tetsuo closed the distance between himself and Ricky, who had only been inching backwards.

Ricky unleashed a middle kick. With only a few pixels to spare, Tetsuo responded with a toe kick. Tetsuo's kick connected, but it was light. Not a counterhit. Tetsuo pressed closer.

Ricky spun away to his right, throwing a backhand as he did. The backhand hit Tetsuo, but Ricky kept retreating. Tetsuo advanced. Ricky shaved another sliver off Tetsuo's health with a crouching punch. It didn't matter. I wasn't worried about crouching punches. If Ricky wanted to knock a few pixels off Tetsuo's health, he was welcome to. Whatever it took to get Tetsuo into position to drive home the combo that would decide the match. Ignoring the chipping he was giving Tetsuo, I closed in and gave the command for a throw. With a head butt, Tetsuo sent Ricky sprawling on the ground. Circling the center of the ring, Tetsuo approached Ricky's prostrate body.

Ricky rolled to the side and regained his feet. He back-dashed to the left. Tetsuo speed-dashed forward and to the left to keep pace. Tracing a broad, 120-degree arc, the two characters slowly grew closer.

Keeping his body low to the ground, Ricky made a spinning foot sweep. Tetsuo launched a low standing spin kick. A counterhit sound FX rang out. The hits landed at the same time, sending both characters flying.

Ricky was the first to rise. He threw a slow but powerful middle punch at Tetsuo as he picked himself up off the ground. Tetsuo blocked. Ricky threw his fastest punch, then another. Canceling out, Ricky kicked low and from the right. The kick landed. Ricky did a speed-dash throw. I gave the throw-break command, but not in time. Tetsuo skidded across the gray textured floor of the arena as Ricky circled toward the middle of the ring.

As he stood, Tetsuo did a middle spin kick. I canceled out of the kick and linked a heel drop. Ricky blocked. He answered with a string of light attacks.

With the exception of his move at the start, Ricky had completely avoided any big moves that could quickly decide the match. That must have been the only point at which I had left myself open to attack. Tetsuo took a few more punches that chipped away at his health. Ricky's health would be lower too, but Tetsuo would still be behind thanks to the large amount of damage he'd taken at the beginning of the match.

Ricky back-dashed. Tetsuo speed-dashed. Immediately canceling, Tetsuo back-dashed and then jump-kicked. The kick landed as a counterhit on the crouching punch Ricky had intended to meet Tetsuo's speed dash. Ricky flew into the air, but not high enough. Tetsuo caught Ricky's falling body with a crouching punch. Canceling out of the move, Tetsuo followed with a low spin kick. The combo didn't land in time. Ricky was on his feet again.

I was running short on time. If no one was KO'd within the time limit, the character with the most remaining health was declared the winner. It was obvious that Ricky intended to keep running away until time ran out.

There's a scene in an old samurai movie where a wise sword master explains how the swordsman who struck first had lost the match before it had begun. The same could be said of fighting games. Waiting for your opponent to attack and then countering whatever he came at you with was a sound strategy. Sound, but not well loved. People who fought like that were often derided as cowards or worse. But this coward was winning.

Ricky didn't always play the waiting game. In the match I'd watched him play the day before, he'd stayed on the offensive the whole time. It was both an indication of how badly he wanted to win this match and how fierce an opponent he considered Tetsuo to be. *Versus Town* was winner-take-all. If you won, it didn't matter what strategy you used to get there. The victory was vindication enough. And Ricky was definitely an ends-justifies-the-means kind of player.

But that wasn't how Tetsuo played. When I was up against an opponent who could only use rock and paper, I threw caution to the wind and flashed scissors. That was the way I had always done it, and it's the way I would always do it, whether in *Versus Town* or anywhere else. If I went with scissors and I lost, so be it. I couldn't go back in time and relive my game against the bear, so I was stuck throwing scissors the rest of my life.

Playing chase with Ricky would hand him the win. To beat him, I had to give him a taste of his own medicine. It would be risky, but nothing ventured, nothing gained.

I pushed the stick once to the right. Tetsuo started walking toward Ricky. Ricky backed away in small, quick steps. Tetsuo kept walking. When he was in range of Ricky's attacks, I didn't block. Completely defenseless, Tetsuo advanced.

My stomach was tied in knots. An attack could come at any moment. All of my attention was focused on the nerves in my fingertips. *You gave yourself the advantage. Let's see you use it. Bring it on.* Step by step, the gap between Tetsuo and Ricky closed.

Ricky's toe shifted a few pixels.

My index finger shot forward.

Ricky attacked with a crouching punch. Tetsuo struck out with his knee. The knee won. The counterhit sound FX played.

Ricky's body was airborne. Tetsuo punched, canceled, and punched again. I linked a kick to the second punch, then canceled into a heel drop. Tetsuo threw a crouching punch, then speed-dashed. He canceled out of the speed dash and delivered a low spin kick. Another speed dash, and then Tetsuo hammered a fist down into Ricky's body as it lay on the ground.

Ricky lay motionless atop a backdrop of sand textures. The sound FX announcing a winner rang out. The match clock was exactly at zero. Turning away from Ricky, who was still lying flat on his back, Tetsuo slowly descended the arena stairs.

Tetsuo won the second and third matches of the day without taking any damage to speak of. That his opponents had reached the second round meant they were good, but they were no match for Tetsuo. Ricky had been a far better fighter than either of them. The broad, flat floor of the arena was boring, and it bred boring competitors. Without having to worry about terrain, all you had to do was input the best countermove, and you would win.

~

A character approached Tetsuo after the third match.

> You're good.

He was wearing a garish gongfu outfit with a large dragon uncoiling across his back. A long braid of hair hung from his balding head. He wore neither headband nor wristband. A middleweight snake boxer, he was familiar to almost everyone in Versus Town—it was Pak.

As the winner of the last tournament, Pak was exempt from the qualifying rounds, so he was here either on a whim or, more likely, to scout potential opponents. Being the best meant more than playing the game well. It required constant effort to gather intelligence on the competition. That was as true of virtual martial arts tournaments as it was of RL contests like the Olympics.

> Ricky's kicking himself right now.
> He put up a good fight.
> Not good enough to beat you. If you're going to turtle, I don't care if your opponent walks up to you without a single block in sight, you have to stick to your strat and keep running.
> You'd have run?
> Nah, I'm more of a rushdown kind of guy. I wouldn't have turtled to begin with. You and I should get along well. I'm looking forward to our match.

> We could fight now, if you want.
> Sorry, I don't street fight.

Just as Ricky had said. I didn't know when the next chance to talk to Pak would come, so I took a shot.

> Why not?
> There's no point.
> I wouldn't say that.
> There's no reason to fight in the streets, and the game devs know it. That's why they implemented forced log outs—to discourage people from engaging in pointless fights. You should've seen the place back in beta. Total madhouse.
> The forced log outs have worked, though.
> Once you get that first ding in a new car, it's all downhill from there. I won't be a part of that.
> What if you ran into Jack in Sanchōme?
> I wouldn't even fight Jack on the streets. No exceptions.
> Don't you want to fight him? See which of you is better?
> Not especially. Now if he entered the tournament, that would be another story. I really am looking forward to our match. Of course we could always play in Shinjuku on the weekends. But I hear you're not a fan.

He walked away before I could reply. I didn't notice until after he had left, but the entire time we were talking he hadn't shifted his posture or made a single gesture. I knew he wasn't a total stranger to JTS, but compared to that bunch, talking to Pak was like talking to a wooden training dummy.

Hashimoto approached me next.

> Congratulations on reaching the finals.
> Thanks.
> I come bearing good news and bad news.
> Let's hear it.

The ninja gave an almost imperceptible nod.

> The tournament brackets have been decided. Should you emerge victorious from all of your matches, you will face Pak in the final round.

> I was just talking to him. He said he was looking forward to the match. Is that supposed to be the good news?

> You are to face the best player in all of Versus Town in a ring prepared specially for the purpose. Surely that qualifies as good news.

> I guess.

The final round of the tournament took place in its own dedicated ring. During the qualifying rounds, at any given time a number of matches might be taking place side by side, but in the finals, all of the matches took place in the same special-built ring.

On the last Saturday in June, from late afternoon into the evening, the sixteen players who advanced to the finals would face each other in a single-elimination tournament. The final match would fall into primetime if this were television. Players logged in to *Versus Town* would be able to watch the match from any perspective they chose, even from the point of view of one of the combatants. During the first season tournament, over 90 percent of the players online had watched the match.

> You don't seem very happy.

> I can't say I am.

Pak and Tetsuo didn't face each other in the brackets until the final round, which meant they both had to survive that long in order to fight. I didn't think Pak would have any trouble making it, but I was less sure about Tetsuo. Only the top sixteen characters reached the finals, which meant whomever Tetsuo went up against would be good. I couldn't say with 100 percent certainty that Tetsuo had what it took to make it.

> Who else am I up against?
> I believe you will be pleased. You face a string of worthy opponents against whom to test your mettle.
> Who?
> If all goes as my whisperers assure me it will, you will face 963 in the first match, Keith in the quarterfinals, and Tanaka in the semifinals.
> The news just goes from bad to worse.

Hashimoto shrugged his polygonal shoulders in a flagrant display of skill.

> You have come far. I do not doubt your success.
> You seem pretty bullish about my prospects.
> What else can I be? If you lose before you face Jack, all my plans will be ruined.
> So what's the real bad news?

It seemed an eternity before the next bubble of text rose above Hashimoto's head.

> Just before I arrived, I received word that Jack defeated Tanaka.

Jack had now fought three of the top four and crushed them all. Masumi, who'd been runner-up in the first season tournament, couldn't stand against him either.

That left only one of the top four. Jack's next target was obvious. His sights would be squarely set on the best snake boxer in Versus Town: Pak.

Tonight's score: 3 wins, 0 losses.

A SOAKING RAIN POURED DOWN ON SHINJUKU.

Tendrils of water streamed across the classroom window one after another. Inside, the air was thick with a steamy, strength-sapping heat. It felt as though half the rain falling from the sky still lingered in the air. As the air conditioner labored it emitted a sound FX laden with hope, but if it was actually cooling anything, I couldn't tell.

2:08 PM. Half-listening as a foreign instructor spoke French, I searched desperately for a cool spot on the desk to rest my head.

As ever, sound FX filled the room. The broken French of a random student the instructor had called on. Snickering from the seats behind me. Strange sounds emerging from the mouth of the foreign instructor. In my experience, native Japanese couldn't understand a word a foreigner spoke in his mother tongue, so why bother trying?

"Wake up, sleepyhead." I felt the tap of Fumiko's 0.7 mm mechanical pencil.

"Cut it out."

"It's the middle of the afternoon. Time to rise and shine."

"I wasn't sleeping." I buried my head in my arm.

"He's gonna call on you if you don't sit up. He knows who you are."

"No way. We all look the same to them."

"How racist of you."

"It's not racist. I can't tell the difference between our English teacher and our French teacher, either."

"That's just you," she said with a grin.

Summer break started at the beginning of July. Exams weren't until after the break, but half of our term papers were due in June. Fumiko's notes were filled top to bottom with row after row of sharply printed text. Copying them was taking much longer than I had expected. During Uemura the Elder's class I was busily copying as Fumiko took notes. The girl was faster than a cheap laser printer.

I needed to finish one and a half papers a day to have them all in on time. Less than ideal. The hunt for Ganker Jack wasn't going much better. Considering the final round of the tournament was tomorrow, I should have been in a better mood than I was.

Fumiko wasn't likely to feel starved for attention during class, so I used every minute I could to steal some much needed rest. I cradled my head in my arms and let myself drift into sleep.

The sound FX announcing the end of class filled my ears. Heaving my bag onto my shoulder I stood, my body still sluggish with exhaustion. Between the papers and the humidity, the bag weighed a ton. I walked out of the classroom with Fumiko clinging lightly to my shirt. We had a little time before our next class, so we went to a lounge—the quiet one without a photocopier.

The lounge was empty. I bought a can of iced coffee from the vending machine and Fumiko got a juice pack. Orange. We sat down side by side in a couple of old plastic chairs.

"Think you can finish your papers?"

"I'll manage."

"How many you have left?"

"Five."

"What have you been doing with all your time?"

"I have reports for classes you're not in. I got those out of the way first."

"That's one night."

"If I were you, maybe."

I stretched in my chair. Fumiko glared at me, a hand on her hip. The silk shirt clinging to her skin caught the light and scattered it through the dense, humid air. I pressed my iced coffee to my forehead. Beads of cold sweat had collected on the sides of the can. Fumiko looked at me with upturned eyes.

"Want me to do them for you?"

"Nah, it's okay."

"Why not?"

"I don't know. I just don't."

"You don't have much time left."

"A week without sleep never killed anybody."

"Didn't do anyone any good either."

"Don't worry, I'll get 'em done. Besides, our professors might be shortsighted, but they're not blind. They'd notice two reports in the same handwriting."

"In that case," Fumiko brushed the hair out of her eyes, "maybe you'll be free tomorrow night?"

"Tomorrow's no good."

"I told you you'd never finish without my help."

"It's not the reports. I already have plans."

"What sort of plans?"

"Plans."

"Are you seeing her?"

"No, these are solo plans."

"Solo? What are you doing?"

"Can we drop it already?" I pulled at my hair. A soft ripping sound FX echoed through the empty lounge. Fumiko's hands were trembling. A growing bead of orange-colored fluid bulged at the tip of the straw thrust into her juice box. Finally the weight was too much for the surface tension and the liquid came spilling out, perfuming the air with a faint citrus aroma.

"Birthdays don't mean anything to you?"

I opened my eyes wide. I knew I hadn't forgotten her birthday. Fumiko was born on December 24. She told me she felt cheated having her birthday so close to Christmas. I had even promised that we'd celebrate Christmas and her birthday separately this year. We were already making plans months in advance.

"Whose birthday?"

"Yours," she squeaked.

"Right."

"What do you mean, 'right'?"

"Guess I forgot."

I had felt something rattling around at the back of my head for a while now. Something that was supposed to happen the last Saturday in June. Mystery solved. Up until now, the only thing I had connected with that Saturday was the *Versus Town* tournament.

Not a lot of guys I knew celebrated their birthdays after they got out of elementary school. By the time you were in junior high, you were lucky if anyone even noticed. Since my birthday fell during finals, it got lost in the noise more than most. My girlfriend in high school never gave me a single birthday present. Not that that stopped her from flying into a rage if I forgot to get her something.

I didn't remember telling Fumiko my birthday. I was turning twenty, but I don't think my parents were even paying attention. Not celebrating my birthday was exactly how we had always celebrated it.

I looked into Fumiko's eyes. "How did you know it was my birthday?"

"It's on your student ID."

"Those glasses must work. Thanks for remembering."

"It's the least I could do." She let out a short, nasal laugh. "And the least you can do is spend it with me."

"I can't."

"Why not?"

"I told you, I've got plans."

"Can't you get out of them? I already made reservations at a restaurant in Ebisu."

"These plans won't change."

"You're sure?"

"I'm sure."

"Just what is it you're doing?"

I'd never enjoyed lying or telling half-truths. That was probably why I said whatever popped into my head. I hadn't deliberately tried to hide the tournament from Fumiko. I just didn't see any point in telling her. But since she'd asked point-blank, I had to be straight with her. Not that this honesty policy had served me all that well in the past, but I wasn't about to change it up now.

So I explained the *Versus Town* tournament to Fumiko. She stared back at me as though I were an alien explaining the propulsion system of my spacecraft.

"You said I was wearing a Naples yellow blouse the day we met, right?"

"Sure, why?"

"You must have had me confused with someone else."

"What?"

"I was wearing blue the day we met. The first time we sat by each other. The first time we talked. Guess you forgot that too."

Sound FX of a juice pack landing on the floor. The lounge door being flung open. Fumiko's footsteps as she walked away.

I opened my eyes. Air rich with the smell of rain streamed in through the open door, caressing the back of my neck. Fumiko's footsteps had already faded to silence. I picked up the juice box she'd thrown to the ground. The straw had come out, and a sticky fluid oozed from the opening.

I always thought this was when a girl slapped a guy. My ex had slapped me plenty of times, hard enough to leave a mark. But Fumiko hadn't done a thing. A flash of sadness swept across her face, and then she was gone.

Fumiko wasn't at our next class. I ducked out and headed for the streets of Shinjuku.

~

Gray light shimmered in the darkness inside the arcade. A mix of blaring music and digital sound FX shook the building. The air conditioning was on overdrive. Still soaking from the rain, I was an ice cube the moment I stepped in.

I had been wandering the streets like I always did, but the relentless rain made a persuasive argument, so finally I fled to the nearest dry spot I could think of. That spot just happened to be the arcade on Kokusai-dōri. Maybe it was because it was Friday, but the place seemed a lot more crowded than the arcade over by Shinjuku Koma Theater.

A snake boxer and a jujutsuka were fighting on a screen at the back of the darkened arena floor. A student on the near side of the machine was playing the jujutsuka. Peering closely at the screen, I saw that the game had just started.

As soon as the round began the snake boxer launched the jujutsuka into the air with a counter and unleashed an E-rank combo on him. The snake boxer timed another counter to land as the jujutsuka regained his feet. The jujutsuka had suffered a perfect defeat in five seconds flat. The snake boxer was good.

A man standing next to me mumbled in a hoarse voice, "Get in line." Apparently there were a lot of people waiting their turn to face the snake boxer.

"My bad," I replied.

I stepped around to the other side of the machine. In front of the screen sat a man with a sharp look in his eye. Not sharp-as-a-tack sharp. This was a look that could cut through a tin can. He wore a threadbare denim jacket and a pair of sandals that hung loosely on his feet.

The man sat expressionless as he manipulated the controls, his body at a slight angle to the console. The whole time I was watching, he stirred only once to cross his legs. Otherwise only his arm moved as it worked the joystick. The sound FX of a dozen games surged through the arcade in a flood of noise, but it all washed over him without a trace. He wasn't in RL. His consciousness was submerged in the world behind the screen.

I recognized his face from a magazine. Of course. It was Friday night at the Kokusai-dōri arcade. This was Pak. Or Pak's player, if you wanted to get technical. It was the first time I had ever seen him in person.

He was as good as they said. The people lined up to play him had all made a special trip down to Shinjuku just for the chance, so it was a safe bet they were better than average themselves. I must have been looking at some of the better players in *Versus Town*, but one challenger fell after another and Pak hadn't taken so much as a scratch. This was even more impressive than the performance I'd seen from Keith in Sanchōme.

The counter at the top of the screen ticked from twenty-eight to twenty-nine. Twenty-nine challengers sent packing with their tails between their legs. Pak's next opponent chose a snake boxer, the same as Pak. Somehow the challenger managed to last to the end of the round, but he couldn't land any good hits of his own. Pak won the first two rounds by Time Out, and it didn't seem like it would be long before the victory count ticked up to thirty.

I broke a thousand-yen bill at the change machine.

To be honest, I didn't want to fight Pak. I would find out who the better player was in the final round of the tournament tomorrow. But I didn't think it was fair to watch Pak fight without giving him the same chance to see Tetsuo. Just because he'd seen me play in the semifinals didn't mean I was about to stoop to spying.

I heard a startled cry from near the game cabinet. It sounded like the man who had told me to stand in line. I hurried back to see what had happened.

The player who lost two straight rounds a moment before had just scored a perfect victory over Pak. It would take more than luck for a reversal like that. Maybe Pak had decided to throw the round.

I turned my attention to the screen as the fourth round began and the two snake boxers slid into motion. Pak put his opponent on the defensive with an attack too quick to be countered, but he blocked every complex cancel-attack Pak threw at him. Hoping to use the recovery time to his advantage, Pak moved in for a throw. His opponent throw-breaked. Pak continued chipping away with small attacks.

A determined expression noticeably absent until now settled on Pak's face. His opponent turned aside each attack he made. He got out of every throw. Dash throws, punch-fakes, tick throws—nothing would take.

It was possible to escape any throw, but only with the right throw break. In theory, you could wait until you saw the throw coming and still have enough time to execute the throw break. In practice, it was virtually impossible to pull it off in the quarter of a second window you had, leaving you to guess which throw your opponent would use and buffer the throw break for that throw. So even if you knew a throw was coming, you never had a 100 percent chance of breaking it. This was the first match I'd ever seen where someone had broken six out of six throws. The challenger won the fourth round with nearly full health.

Pak twisted his neck from side to side, creating loud popping sound FX. The fifth and final round began.

Pak input commands with blinding speed. There were no throws in his arsenal this round. He was coming at his opponent with only rock and paper, hoping to cow him with brute force, but it didn't change a thing. It was an even match, and the challenger's health dropped in small, measured increments.

In the end, the fifth round went to Pak. He had come from behind to win the match.

I heard a familiar voice behind me. "He doesn't stand a chance." It was the bat lady. Lui. Hashimoto. It struck me as odd that someone who lived in Kabuki-chō would make the trip all the way to an arcade on the west side of the station. As usual her face showed no trace of makeup. She lit up when she noticed me.

"Who?" I asked.

"The old man."

I peered around to see a small boy seated on the other side of the cabinet. Some elementary school kid on his way home from school. He cast one last rueful look at the screen and stood up.

"Don't tell me."

"Yep, that's the grandson."

"He could play with both hands behind his back and that poor guy wouldn't have a prayer."

"My thoughts exactly." Lui shrugged. "The things people do for their grandkids." She motioned at Pak with her small, pointed chin. "You gonna have a go?"

"No, I just wanted to get out of the rain. I can play *VT* online. Why bother with an arcade? Holy ground or not, I'm not sure what Pak sees in this place."

"This is where it has to be," she muttered, more to herself than to me.

"What do you mean?"

"This is the only place a win feels like a win. At least that's how I think he sees it. This may not be the original 'holy ground,' but it's close enough."

"A win's a win. What difference does it make where it happens?"

"It's not the place itself. When he's here, they're together. He's Pak and himself at the same time."

"How's that any different from playing online?"

"For some people, it's different."

"I think you lost me."

"So you're one of those." She sounded disappointed.

Next thing I knew, Pak was standing beside us. He'd beaten

the player in line behind the old man's grandson and played through the rest of the computer opponents. Sitting down he had seemed paper-thin. Standing he looked as though he might blow away if the air conditioning hit him just right.

"Want to play?" His voice was much higher than I had expected.

"No thanks."

"Oh, all right." He went back to the game.

Eardrum-rattling music filled the arcade. A perfect harmony of sound FX, real and artificial, engulfed us.

"I'm sorry about the other day," Lui offered.

"Don't worry about it. It's not your fault."

"Things been rough since then?"

"Even if they were—and I'm not saying they are—that still doesn't make it your fault."

"You two are closer than I thought."

"If we were close, we wouldn't fight."

"Don't be so sure. It's not easy figuring out if someone's special," she said. "Two perfect strangers struggling to understand each other. It's finding out the differences that lets them fight."

"This from experience?"

"Maybe it is." She shrugged again. "Like magnets: opposites attract. People are the same. Everyone has their flaws, their quirks. Rub them together, you get friction. It's the places where they're different that locks them together." Lui paused to wind a strand of red-brown hair around her finger. "Our shop's not open yet, but maybe you could drop by."

We walked in the rain from the station's west gate to Kabuki-chō. The building Lui's shop was in looked exactly as it had the first time I saw it, lost somewhere between up-and-coming and down-and-out on the outskirts of the entertainment district. The aura of desolation surrounding it reminded me a little of the JTS Saloon.

The laser at the front of the shop was doing its best to spell

out the name of the establishment on the wet asphalt, but the
water pooled in the uneven ground scattered the light, making
it difficult to read. The oscillator was still broken, warping
the store's name and casting blue beams unpredictably up and
down the street.

Lui leaned back against the door of the shop. "Still looking
for that blue cat?"

"Uh, yeah, I guess. It's Fumiko who's looking, really."

"That right?" Lui nodded to herself. "So what you're searching for isn't as important as the search."

"You don't think she wants to find it?"

"I didn't say that. That's the point of the whole thing, but—
how can I put it. It's like getting a can of peaches when you're
sick."

"Peaches?"

"No canned peaches from Mom when you came down with
a cold?"

"It was Jell-O, actually. Just a batch of the instant powder
stuff, but that was fine by me."

"Canned peaches, Jell-O—it's all the same. You want to get
over your cold, but you know that when you do, no more
special treats. See where I'm going?"

"I've got the idea."

"Good. Now take a look at that wall."

Lui raised her arm and pointed with an outstretched finger.
As she did, she lifted her cloak-or-was-it-a-shawl, looking for
all the world like a bat with one upraised wing. Her long claw
indicated a concrete block covered with moss.

Light burst from the broken laser. A blue cat appeared on
the concrete, then vanished.

"No way."

"Getting there is half the fun. Now here you are."

The path of the laser bent again with a soft pop, and the
blue cat flickered to life on the concrete block. If you looked
closely, it was obviously part of the store's name distorted out

of shape. But for a brief moment, it was a blue cat sitting on the street corner.

"Not the usual stuff urban legends are made of, but it seems to have caught on. Your girlfriend isn't looking for the cat. She's looking for someone to look for the cat with." Lui lit a cigarette. The laser beam danced in the smoke.

"Like Hashimoto, maybe?"

"Like Hashimoto how?"

"Maybe Hashimoto isn't looking for Jack, he's just looking for people to look for Jack with him."

"Interesting thought." She took a long drag on her cigarette and let it burn down another seven millimeters. "I can't really say. I don't know how to get inside the head of a virtual character like Hashimoto."

Lui hadn't brought me here to visit her shop. For some reason, she decided it was time to show me the cat. The first time I asked her about it she'd gone out of her way to hide it from me. I don't know what had changed her mind now. Answerless, I headed home.

On the train, my thoughts kept going to that kid. I envisioned him fighting Tetsuo, gracefully breaking one throw after another in time to the sound FX of the wheels as they raced over the tracks. No matter how many times I tried, I couldn't land a throw on him. The kid had a smirk textured on his face.

An email appeared on my cell phone. Just two words: "Drop dead."

I switched on my music, but the batteries had died.

~

I called Fumiko from the platform at Mizuhodai. She didn't waste any time getting to the cross-examination.

"Where have you been?"

"The arcade."

"Again?"

"You weren't in class."

"I came late."

"You weren't there when I was there."

"You didn't think to wait and see if I'd show up? Or maybe follow me when I walked off?"

"It didn't seem like the thing to do."

"What's wrong with you?"

"Nothing," I said. "This is pretty normal for me, actually."

"'Does not play well with others'? Is that what they wrote on your report card back in elementary school?"

"Junior high and high school too."

I heard Fumiko's sigh over the phone. "At least tell me you feel bad about it."

"I do."

"Really? With you, it's hard to tell."

"I guess."

"Just guess?"

With each dodge of her questions I could feel the thread that bound us together fray a bit more. My words were converted to signals that traveled through space and cables just to reach her. But then those emotionless signals were turned back into words, and maybe something got lost in the translation.

I moved my ear off the warm handset.

"Are you even listening?"

"I'm listening."

"Don't you have anything to say?"

"I'm saying it."

I thought about it for a moment. It wasn't easy, explaining the maelstrom raging inside me, devouring my life. Tetsuo fought for the sake of fighting. If there was any other reason, I didn't know what it was. Right now, all I had room for in my head was the *Versus Town* tournament. I was even playing out fights in my head while on the toilet.

I couldn't put into words the reason I was letting this one thing consume my life. But that didn't mean Fumiko didn't have a right to know. So I tried to find the words for something I didn't even understand myself. It was grueling and exhausting, but she deserved that much.

Fumiko broke the silence. "You really are Fast Eddie."

"Who?"

"That character Paul Newman played."

"Sorry? Paul Newman?"

"*The Hustler*, remember? We talked about it before."

"I can never remember foreign names. Not on the first try, at least."

"That's because you don't pay attention to me."

"Don't start."

"You just nod your head to get through the conversation."

"That's not true."

"A lot more people know about Paul Newman than the president of Hudson Soft's trains."

"Probably."

"Your knowledge base is off. Way off."

"You're right."

"Eddie treats his girlfriend in *The Hustler* bad too. She dies at the end, you know."

"I didn't, actually."

"I don't plan on dying anytime soon."

"That's a relief."

"You use words to keep people at a distance."

"Sorry. I don't know any other way to talk."

The line fell silent. I didn't know what else to say. I'd already said everything. I wasn't going to lie to her, and I didn't want to repeat myself.

"Asshole."

Ten seconds later, the line went dead.

I'd forgotten to tell her I'd found the blue cat.

I stood on the platform staring at my cell phone for a couple of seconds before walking out into the rain-slick streets. In the dim glow of car taillights and streetlamps I walked over to the video rental store in front of the station. That night I watched *The Hustler* for the first time.

Fast Eddie was, as the title suggests, a pool hustler. He was a real bastard who stole money from unsuspecting marks, took them for all they had, and then left them to fend for themselves. He dreamed of beating pool legend Minnesota Fats and didn't care about anything else. Fumiko had it right; he sacrificed his friends, his girlfriend, everything he had for pool.

He was just like me, standing in the corner beside the train doors. He didn't want to play Minnesota Fats to win ten thousand dollars. The money was nothing to him. There was something inside, some reason only he knew, that drove him to do it. Hell, maybe he didn't even know what his reason was, but he knew it was there. For him, it was the most important thing in the world.

Tetsuo had to see things in *Versus Town* through to the end. It wasn't about anyone else. It was something I had to prove to myself.

Nearly three weeks had passed since I met Fumiko. I couldn't say whether she was my girlfriend or not. We were always together at school, but that didn't amount to much. Things in RL were more complicated than that. There was no way of knowing what flags you had to trip to make a relationship work. Maybe I was the only one who felt that our search for the blue cat was leading the two of us somewhere special.

I considered myself lucky to have met Fumiko, but did she feel the same?

Outside the rain poured down on the city.

ANOTHER SUNNY DAY IN VERSUS TOWN.
The same scenery filled the TV screen. The same turquoise blue sky. The same butter roll clouds. The same textures covering the ground and walls. Today only one thing was different: Tetsuo stood in the middle of the tournament ring.

A character in a suit with a mic approached Tetsuo as he stepped out of the ring.

> The karateka Tetsuo, ladies and gentlemen. Congratulations on making it to the semifinals. I think it's no understatement to say you've been on fire.
> So far so good.
> You've hardly taken any damage at all.
> That's more luck than anything.
> You knew that your opponents were members of the so-called top four?
> Yeah.
> So how do you feel?
> Pretty much like I always do, I guess.
> You must keep a pretty cool head then.

It was two hours into the finals of the second season tournament. Tetsuo had scored an almost perfect win over 963 in the first match, and just now he had defeated Keith. Tetsuo's match was the last of the quarterfinals.

The interviewer who had just finished talking with Tetsuo was one of the sysadmins. The chat they'd just had would be broadcast to all of the players watching the tournament.

The first three quarterfinal spots were held by Tanaka,

an eagle claw, Tetsuo, a karateka, and Pak, a snake boxer. A nameless snake boxer had claimed the last spot. There was a thirty-minute break before the quarterfinals began.

Having gone through the motions with the interviewer, Tetsuo took refuge in the prep room set aside for the contestants. Dressed in full ninja regalia, Hashimoto was waiting in silence by the entrance.

> Congratulations.
> Thanks.
> I see I was right.
> Don't start. I got lucky is all.
> Is that humility I detect? Next thing I know rain clouds will be gathering over Versus Town.

Hashimoto looked up at the ceiling with deliberate nonchalance. Tetsuo shrugged.

> So, find anything?

Everyone who made it to the finals had already earned a reputation in the arena. But with the exception of a win against Tanaka, the nameless snake boxer who found himself in the quarterfinals was a relative unknown with no record to speak of. Hashimoto had suspected this dark horse challenger might be Ganker Jack.

> Alas, no.
> Oh well.
> He came to Versus Town around when you did, but he arrives too early in the day for anyone to have taken note.
> Early to bed, early to rise.
> But how healthy and how wise?
> That's the question.
> I still smell the proverbial rat.

> I'm not so sure.
> He IS a skilled throw breaker.
> Oh, he's good, but not 100 percent good.
> No one can break throws 100 percent of the time.
> True that.
> Still, he must have some weakness.
> Only one way to find out.
> You sound every bit the comic book hero.

I could have sworn I saw a smile flash across the immutable textures of Hashimoto's face.

According to Hashimoto's grapevine, viewership for the tournament was over 90 percent. If the mystery snake boxer really was Jack, he would have a huge audience to witness his victory.

Something told me Jack wouldn't be caught dead in a situation like that. If all he wanted to do was defeat Pak, he could have entered the tournament like everyone else and been done with it. Why spend all that time lurking in the shadows of Sanchōme waiting for an opponent that might not even log in? No, Ganker Jack was driven by that same nameless force that drove Hashimoto to role-play and Tetsuo to obsess over fighting in a make-believe world.

> Jack would never enter the tournament.
> Not as Jack, at any rate.
> What do you mean?
> Perhaps he is like me. Now, I am ninja, but I do not always walk in shadow. Jack may not always show the same colors we have seen.

Hashimoto let down his mask to relax at JTS in a tuxedo. Maybe it wasn't impossible to think that when Ganker Jack let down his mask, he fought in tournaments.

> I don't know about him, but I just want to fight the best.
> Of course you do.
> What are you going to do if that snake boxer is Jack?
> Nothing.
> Nothing?
> The hunt is its own reward. In this town, what do we seek if not reward?
> Always the philosopher.
> I am ninja, and there are inquiries to be made. If you'll excuse me.

Hashimoto sprinted off.

There was still some time before the next match, so Tetsuo made his way to the arena door.

Tetsuo arrived at the wall dividing Nichōme and Sanchōme.

The speakers emitted a soft hum. There were no sound FX here. Huge polygons made up the buildings, and even though these were the same graphics that brought Sanchōme to life, here they seemed sterile and dead.

Since he started spending all his time at JTS, Tetsuo seldom came to Nichōme. He didn't even feel at home in the arena the way he once had. Today there was something he wanted to try that brought him to the wall.

Only lightweight characters could freely jump the E-rank wall surrounding the city. Middleweights like Tetsuo needed something to act as a springboard.

After watching Jack slip through my fingers, I had practiced again and again until I mastered using overturned steel drums to boost myself over walls. Unfortunately, overturned steel drums were strictly features of Sanchōme; if you needed one in Itchōme, you were out of luck. All of which meant that for now, the wall-scaling shortcut from Sanchōme to Itchōme was a one-way trip.

Taking Main Street through Itchōme and using every

shortcut in the book, it took precisely five minutes and forty-five seconds to reach the JTS Saloon. No matter how much they prettied up Sanchōme, it didn't take long to get tired of the scenery. It took less than one minute from log-in to the arena, so if you could find a shortcut to Sanchōme behind the arena, you'd be shaving a lot of time off your commute.

Tetsuo ran along the wall that divided the virtual city. In Itchōme the arena stood a good distance from the wall, but in Nichōme they were right on top of each other. At the spot where the arc of the arena came closest to the wall, it might just be possible to use the polygons of the building to propel a middleweight character like Tetsuo over the wall.

I adjusted my perspective, viewing the building from a variety of angles. I found a window frame in just the right place. It was set slightly into the wall, so although it wouldn't be possible to climb up onto it, it would make for a solid foothold.

Tetsuo backed up against the dividing wall and started running at a right angle toward the face of the arena. Two and a half steps out, he jumped, followed by a high jump as his foot connected with the window frame. If it worked, the triangle jump would propel Tetsuo over the wall.

Tetsuo traced a wide parabola in the air, narrowly missing the top of the wall. But not in the direction he'd intended. He crashed into its side and slid unceremoniously back to the ground.

I repeated the attempt several times, each time adjusting my timing, but Tetsuo always came up just short of the top. A lightweight character like Hashimoto could probably have made the jump without even needing to air-block.

Before I knew it, the digital clock on my DVR read 6:20 PM. Just ten minutes before the semifinals started. If I didn't get back soon, I'd be late. I started to retrace my steps along the periphery of the arena.

On my way back, something caught my eye—a light pole at the edge of the screen.

It stood exactly one jump distant from the window frame, but was just a hair closer to the wall. I decided to give it a try. Tetsuo backed up to give himself room for a running start.

This time, Tetsuo ran toward the window frame at a 45-degree angle. Two and a half steps from the wall, he jumped. Tetsuo air-blocked to shift his position and give his feet purchase on the window frame, then immediately high-jumped off the frame. His new trajectory sent him toward the light pole. The instant before he struck the pole Tetsuo performed another air block, kicking off the pole to complete the triangle jump.

Tetsuo's body traced a wide arc through the air. This time, he rose just a little higher.

The instant before hitting the wall, I gave the command to air-block. At the height of the arc, Tetsuo's body twisted to the side. The polygons of his body caught on the top of the wall. Another air block shifted Tetsuo's center of gravity, sending his body careening over the top of the wall.

Sanchōme sprawled around Tetsuo.

Nichōme it was not. The clean, tidy streets had been replaced by a gritty, polygonal slum.

I laughed. Just a giggle at first, then louder until at last I was roaring in spite of myself. Tetsuo couldn't laugh, so I had to laugh hard enough for the both of us. In a way, it was almost too easy. The E-rank wall towering over Tetsuo seemed smaller than it once had.

Using this shortcut, I could probably trim three minutes off the time it took me to get to JTS from log-in. It was even trickier than jumping off a rolling steel drum. It was a small miracle I'd made the jump on my first try. Maybe it really was my lucky day.

There wasn't much time, so Tetsuo started looking for some polygons that would get him back over the wall. The only thing nearby was a small can of kerosene—too small for a springboard. Tetsuo moved his search to the next street. If he kept his opponent waiting too long, he'd be disqualified.

Someone appeared at the edge of the screen as it began to scroll. Whoever it was had leapt over the same E-rank wall Tetsuo had just scaled and come sliding to the ground in the same location.

One thing was for certain: it wasn't Hashimoto.

He wore a black tank top and black leather pants. A white skull was dyed into the texture on his back. There was a black wristband on his forearm. Where his eyes and mouth should have been there was only a sinister mask, its grin done up like those designs the Americans painted on the noses of their bombers during the war. He looked like a middleweight snake boxer.

Tetsuo turned to face the masked man. He was ahead and 45 degrees to the left. Three steps away, Tetsuo stopped.

A bubble of text appeared above the man's head.

> Karateka. Are you Tetsuo?

With my left hand still on the stick, I pecked at the keyboard with my right.

> I am.
> Let's fight.
> Are you Ganker Jack?
> That's what they call me, anyway.
> Sorry, I've got a tournament to get back to.

I looked around the screen. The only thing on the ground was that can of kerosene. Tetsuo would need more than that to make it back over the wall. It didn't occur to me to cut my connection and log in again.

> You running?
> There's the tournament.
> So that's why you're here. Couldn't take the buzzing of the flies back at the arena? Had to hit the quiet city streets?

> The semifinals are about to start.
> So?
> If I beat Tanaka, I'm in the finals. Beat Pak, and I'm No. 1.
> You really believe that?
> What?
> Why do you fight?
> I fight to be the best.
> Then you're wasting your time with Pak.
> He's last year's champion.
> You really think whoever wins in that little ring is the best?
> Why not?
> In boxing, it's a boxer. In fencing, it's a fencer. There's a best for every set of rules. We don't need an arena to tell us who the best is. Whoever wins in the arena is the champion of the arena. The best in town is the best in town.

Tetsuo and Jack stood in a small alley in Sanchōme. All around them sprawled the slums of the city. The kerosene can rested at the edge of the screen. They were in a virtual space. A city without electricity or gas. Without hospitals or post offices. It was a make-believe city populated with make-believe beings. And Tetsuo had a question for Ganker Jack.

> Why do you gank people?
> Not the first time I've been asked.

Jack walked slowly to one side, making a clear path for Tetsuo.

> I picked you for a reason. But if you got your heart set on that tournament, I won't keep you from it. Go beat Pak. Let everybody tell you how great you are.

The clock on my DVR read 6:31 PM. If I hurried, I could make it to the ring in about two minutes. Tetsuo and Tanaka's match started after Pak's, so if I left now, I still had time.

I knew Tetsuo was good.

Tetsuo practiced combos on training dummies. Tetsuo explored the back alleyways of Sanchōme. Tetsuo could kick off a rolling steel drum to jump an E-rank wall. Tetsuo hunted Jack. Tetsuo entered the tournament. Tetsuo, Tetsuo, Tetsuo... I was Tetsuo, but for some reason, at that moment of all times, I couldn't get Fumiko out of my mind.

Fumiko and I were two very different people. We thought differently, we lived differently. We had different likes and dislikes. We didn't even take notes at the same speed. We could see eye to eye on an intellectual level, but we were as different as night and day.

But that was what kept us together.

I'd fallen into the habit of adjusting my life to suit hers. I sacrificed sleep to wake up earlier. I went to lectures I had no intention of listening to. I searched for the blue cat she was supposed to be looking for even harder than she did. I felt as though everything I did had to mesh with her worldview. But that was a mistake. We fought because we had different sets of values, and that wasn't something worth fighting over. It didn't matter that we didn't share a single common interest. It was enough that I was by her side, and she was by mine. And that's why I cared for her. No, that's why I loved her. It finally made sense. I could finally admit it to myself.

I loved her, and because I loved her I had to be the person that she loved. I had to follow through with what I had begun. I had to fight. That was the person she had fallen for. If I ran away, if I turned back now, then that person would cease to exist.

I felt the mist around my heart burn away. Funny that I should realize all this online, talking to someone I didn't know in a side alley of a city that didn't even exist in RL.

Because I couldn't find the words to say the only important thing there was to say, Fumiko and I had missed our chance. Or maybe life was nothing more than a series of missed chances.

I felt a laugh rise in my throat. I tried to swallow it, but it came spilling out all the same. It was a good thing I was in Versus Town when it did. Here my laugh remained a secret thing. Unless it affected the stick I held or the buttons I pressed, Jack would never know. If he had, he'd probably think I was certifiably deranged.

If Fumiko and I were complete opposites, Tetsuo and Jack were two peas in a pod. They dreamed the same dream and lived by the same code. The spot they were vying for wasn't a spot on the winner's platform, it was lurking somewhere down in the slums of Sanchōme. And it wasn't big enough for the two of them. In the small hours of the night, while ordinary people lay asleep in their beds, Tetsuo and Jack scoured the darkest corners of this virtual town looking for it.

Tetsuo didn't need to prove his skill to anyone. Neither did Jack. They knew their skill, and that was enough. This was a choice I couldn't get wrong. To be true to who I was, I knew who Tetsuo had to fight.

I looked into the screen and took a slow, deep breath. I flicked out a command with the stick. Tetsuo dropped into a fighting stance.

I input another command as I typed. Broken down into packets of light my command sped through fiber optic cables to the game's servers for processing, the resulting calculations reduced again to packets that boomeranged back to my console. After a delay lasting a mere fifteenth of a second, Tetsuo adjusted his white headband.

> Let's rock.
> Music to my ears.
> You wanna get us started?
> After you.
I counted slowly to three.

My fingers flashed over the controls, giving the command for a speed dash. Tetsuo covered the three and a half steps between himself and Jack in a headlong rush. I canceled out of a punch into an elbow, then canceled again into a throw.

The throw landed. Tetsuo grabbed Jack by the nape of the neck. Jack brushed Tetsuo's hand away, causing them both to spin 45 degrees around each other before coming to a halt. The two characters stood facing each other a step and a half apart.

Maybe throws weren't going to work on Jack after all. I put in a slight delay before inputting the command, so even with a throw break in his buffer my throw should have made it through. Should have. But Jack was responding to the throws as they appeared on-screen. It shouldn't have been possible, but someone with superhuman reflexes just might be able to pull it off.

Jack stepped forward and to the right. Tetsuo advanced, throwing his fastest punch as he did. Jack dodged to the left. Then he turned his back against the E-rank wall.

Tetsuo rushed at Jack. Tetsuo threw a punch, followed immediately by a crouching punch. Jack blocked both, then went on the offensive. He launched a roundhouse kick, canceled it. Jack turned and leapt toward the wall at a roughly 90-degree angle. He air-blocked, then launched a flying kick at Tetsuo as he came out of the triangle jump off the wall. I couldn't block in time, and Tetsuo took the full force of the attack.

Jack closed in on Tetsuo as he lay sprawled on the ground. Tetsuo rolled to one side, gaining some distance. Jack launched a roundhouse kick as Tetsuo got back on his feet. Tetsuo blocked. Jack canceled out of a spin kick into a crouching punch. Tetsuo's health fell.

Jack fell back. Tetsuo followed, canceling out of a punch-kick combo into a speed dash. Normally this was when Tetsuo would have gone for a throw, but he went with a low spin kick instead. The attack caught Jack in the leg, throwing him off balance. Tetsuo jabbed with his elbow as he advanced, but Jack had already recovered, giving him just enough time to block the attack.

I grunted in frustration.

If you could rule out being thrown, the only things you had to watch out for were midair combos off a counter. Catching Ganker Jack in midair without throwing him would be even harder than I'd imagined. If Tetsuo's arsenal was reduced to rock and paper, then the outcome was more or less decided before the fight had even begun.

But Pak had done it. On holy ground in a Shinjuku arcade, Pak had won using nothing but rock and paper. Pak, who even then had thousands of eyes on him as he competed in the finals, had pulled it off.

I had to get out of the open. Tetsuo darted into the thick of Sanchōme. Only a split second behind, Jack gave chase.

Another figure appeared suddenly on the screen. The character had scaled the E-rank wall and landed in roughly the same place Tetsuo and Jack had come tumbling down.

I reached for my keyboard. Words bubbled over Tetsuo's head.

> Wait. Someone's here.
>You didn't show for a quarterfinal match. Someone must've gotten curious.
> What now? Keep fighting?
> I ain't stopping. If they're looking for you, we'll go somewhere they won't find you. How's the back side of Sanchōme sound?
> JTS?
> We'll finish this there.
> Don't get lost.
> I'll be there, don't you worry.

Jack melted into the alleys of Sanchōme. Tetsuo just stood there, hoping to conceal the fact that they'd been fighting only moments before.

The man who had scaled the wall wore a deep blue ninja outfit. On his feet was a pair of jet-black tabi. He was a lightweight character, a jujutsuka. Versus Town's very own ninja, Hashimoto.

Hashimoto approached with his usual gait. He turned to face Tetsuo, 45 degrees ahead and to the left. He stood three and a half steps away, just out of Tetsuo's dash-throw range.

> Well done.
> What did I do?
> You flushed out the fox.

Hashimoto's slightly out-of-place role-playing was reassuringly familiar.

> Yeah.
> Then my suspicion was correct. The window in which he could safely contact you was small.
> So you saw this coming. Pretty sharp.
> I will take over from here. Make your way back to the arena.

I figured Hashimoto would say as much, but it didn't make it any easier to hear. Tetsuo stood there, an empty text bubble hanging over his head.

> Why do you hesitate?
> Sorry. I can't do that.
> Pak will be expecting you.
> I don't care. Pak's not important anymore.
> I was under the impression being the best in Versus Town was the object of your quest. Do you intend to let this chance slip away?
> My fight is somewhere else. Out here, in the back alleys.
> The arena is also a part of this town.
> No. So long as Pak's player exists in Shinjuku as Pak's player, I won't find him where I'm looking. I know that now.

But we've already been over this.

> I have no recollection of that conversation.

> Drop the act. I know you don't like mixing the real with the virtual, but this is important. You keep your two personas as separate as anyone, so you should understand. We talked about this at the arcade in Shinjuku.

> Alas, you are mistaken. I can no longer go to Shinjuku.

> What is lying about it now going to serve?

> Ninja never lie. I live in Hokkaido.

> What?

Hashimoto stood there, three and a half steps away, his expression unchanging. A face made only of textures couldn't change its expression.

> Tetsuo, is it not possible you have confused me with another? It is true that my player—that I—have been to Shinjuku. But now I am fled north. I live in exile.

> Then you aren't Lui?

> Alas, this person named Lui is not known to me.

He stood there beneath a bubble of text. Tetsuo's bubble still held his last question.

I tried to think back on our conversations. I couldn't believe it. Lui had never said she was Hashimoto. In fact, she'd never said anything about who she was. All she had said was, "Alas, I am sworn to secrecy." With those words and a wink, she had me hook, line and sinker. Lui knew so much about *Versus Town* that it never even occurred to me she could be anyone else. When I thought about it, it made sense though. Anyone who had ever been to JTS would know who Hashimoto was.

The things she said in Shinjuku could have been said by anyone. There was nothing that only Hashimoto would have known. Looking back, it actually made even more sense coming from someone that wasn't Hashimoto. A role-player like the person who played Hashimoto would never suggest that an arcade in Shinjuku was more important to Pak than Versus Town itself. Whoever it was would also have had to see what I had seen. Spent hours on end going where I had gone. In all of Versus Town, there was only one other character I could think of who fit the bill.

A shiver ran up my spine. It traveled through my shoulders and arms before reaching my hand and shaking the stick. That tiny tremble was reduced to a digital signal and sent to the server.

Tetsuo moved. Hashimoto tensed, ready to fight.

> You role-play a ninja, right?
> Technically no. My player role-plays this character, and this character role-plays a ninja.
> That's what you said about Ganker Jack.
> Because that is what I believe.

Hashimoto had part of it right, but he had missed something. Whoever played Jack was role-playing. But if the person playing Jack was who I thought it was, they were role-playing in RL as sure as Hashimoto was role-playing here. A real wolf in sheep's clothing. Jack was the true essence of the player, the inner self unleashed.

Or maybe everyone in RL was role-playing. To make it from one day to the next, we donned our masks. A way of finding a place for ourselves in a world where we had no place.

> Is something amiss?
> I get it now.
> What is it that you get?
> The reason I have to fight Ganker Jack. The reason I can't back down.

Hashimoto folded his arms. I realized he looked exactly as he had the first time we met in front of the wall in Sanchōme.

> If you insist on this course of action, Tetsuo, I will have no choice but to stop you. What you should be doing is fighting Pak while I uncover Jack's true identity. Do that and we both win.

> Jack is Jack. That much I know.

> I don't understand.

> You're welcome to watch us fight.

> In my estimation, you stand a good chance of defeating him. A proposition that would cause me no end of trouble.

> Then we have a problem. There's only one chair, and when the music stops, I plan to be the one sitting. Whatever it takes.

> I would prefer to resolve this peacefully, but alas, that is not the way of things here.

> I hope there aren't any hard feelings.

> As do I.

Hashimoto leapt into the air—a high jump that took him over Tetsuo's head. He had just reduced the gap between them from three and a half steps to zero. My fingers moved at once. Tetsuo rolled forward, narrowly dodging the attack. Hashimoto landed.

Tetsuo turned in time to see Hashimoto sprint away. He wasn't trying to run; he meant for me to follow.

Looking back to ensure Tetsuo was behind him, Hashimoto wove his way deeper into the maze of streets. The two characters worked their way toward the heart of Sanchōme, exchanging small tit-for-tat attacks as they went.

They came to a narrow intersection. A steel drum lay on the ground. Hashimoto kicked the drum at Tetsuo, who kicked it right back. As it bore down on him, Hashimoto hopped over the drum with a flying kick at Tetsuo. Tetsuo blocked. While Hashimoto recovered from the attack, Tetsuo tried to throw him, but Hashimoto managed to throw-break.

His hunt for Jack had led Hashimoto back and forth through all of Versus Town; he knew Sanchōme as well as anyone. And although Ricky had beaten him, he was by no means a bad fighter. His moves walked a fine line between daring and foolish, but no doubt that was all part of his plan.

A middleweight character like Tetsuo could never catch a lightweight like Hashimoto running at full speed. A common lightweight tactic was to gain some distance, launch a few quick attacks, and then pull away again, slowly chipping away at their opponent as they did. All well and good for Hashimoto, less than ideal for Tetsuo.

Hashimoto had no intention of defeating Tetsuo. All he needed to do was keep himself alive while lowering Tetsuo's health enough so that Jack could take care of the rest. Once Jack defeated Tetsuo, Hashimoto could follow him and discover once and for all who he was.

Tetsuo's health had already dropped a noticeable amount. In the process Tetsuo had inflicted about three times as much damage on Hashimoto, but in a battle like this it scarcely mattered. As soon as this fight was over, the deadliest person in Sanchōme was waiting for Tetsuo. Even going against him at full health, Ganker Jack was nearly unstoppable. Knowing this, reading Hashimoto was easy. He was staging the fight to shave off as much of Tetsuo's health as possible. So even if it meant taking some damage in the process, Tetsuo couldn't let Hashimoto escape.

Tetsuo rolled forward. As soon as his feet were back beneath him, he jumped. Kicking off a nearby wall, he executed a triangle jump, sailing high over Hashimoto's head. Flying through the air as he was, Tetsuo was wide open to attack. I focused my entire attention on the joystick gripped between my fingers.

Hashimoto took the bait. He came at Tetsuo with a somersault kick, a big move. I gave the command to air-block just in time. Tetsuo landed safely on the ground just as Hashimoto was recovering from the failed attack.

From here on out it was a game of real-time rock-paper-scissors. Only in this game, you could wait to see what your opponent threw. You could change your own move midswing. You could even read your opponent's move before he made it. It was all in the rules. To win, you had to be able to feint and trick your opponent into revealing his hand. Tetsuo canceled out of a punch-kick combo into a speed dash, and went straight from that into a throw. The head butt Hashimoto received in the melee sent him crashing to the ground.

Tetsuo closed in on his fallen friend. He speed-dashed again, then canceled. Before Tetsuo had even begun to move, I buffered the command to send him circling in at an angle to the left.

As he regained his feet, Hashimoto launched a spin kick. I saw it coming with only a few pixels to spare and gave the command for a flying knee. The sound FX of the knee connecting played in my speakers. I had landed a counter.

Tetsuo caught Hashimoto's body with his fastest punch. I canceled and punched again. I tacked a kick onto the second punch, and then canceled out mid-combo to chain a heel drop onto the end. Hashimoto's body slammed into the ground. I landed a crouching punch as he bounced back into the air and then queued a speed dash. Canceling out of the speed dash I threw a low spin kick. I speed-dashed again. Tetsuo drove a fist down into Hashimoto's prone body.

Hashimoto grew still. After a few seconds, he faded from the screen.

In RL, somewhere far to the north, Tetsuo still appeared on the television screen of Hashimoto's player. I could talk to him if I wanted to. But I had nothing to say to Hashimoto in his virtual world.

I tapped the stick twice. Tetsuo ran.

~

I soon arrived at a familiar place. Weathered boards textured the walls. A pair of swinging wooden doors hung in the entrance. Off to one side stood a lone wooden barrel. Two thick wooden columns rose in front of the building, and above them rested an old sign whose polygons were painstakingly placed at the slightest of angles.

The JTS Saloon looked as it always had, and it had never looked better.

> You're late.

Jack stood with arms crossed in front of the swinging doors.

> I had some loose ends to tie up.
> I thought the lure of the winner's podium had gotten to you.
> Not likely. This town doesn't need a winner's podium.
> Got that right.
> We're the only people that need to know who's better.
> You finally see.
> I was curious about one thing, though.
> Yeah?
> ~~Is your player named Lui?~~

I deleted that last question before pressing ENTER. It didn't matter if the bat lady I'd met in Shinjuku was Jack or not. Maybe Jack's player was that insanely good elementary school kid who challenged Pak. Maybe it was someone else entirely. I didn't need to know. That sort of information was useless here.

There were no spectators. There would be no record of the outcome. There was only the screen and the joystick in my hand. A handful of buttons. A game console wired to the net. That was all that separated us. The image of Jack on my screen was the sum total of what I needed to know about him, and the image of Tetsuo on his screen was all he needed to know about me.

> You going to make me start this again?
> If you think you can.

I counted slowly to three.

I input the speed-dash command. Tetsuo slipped past Jack and threw himself through the swinging doors.

Inside, the saloon was dark and empty. There was no trace of Ben the bartender or Masumi. When Hashimoto lost the street fight he had been forced to log out. Ricky would be watching the tournament. It was too early for the other regulars to be logged in.

Tetsuo vaulted onto the bar. Jack came running into the saloon in time with the swinging doors. My fingers raced over the controls. Tetsuo turned to face Jack and launched a standing flying kick. Jack did a forward roll to dodge. As he rose to his feet, he threw a middle spin kick. His foot struck a table fixed to the ground, knocking him off balance.

Tetsuo dashed forward. He threw a knee. The counterhit sound FX played.

Jack's body flew into the air and struck the ceiling. Tetsuo kneed him again as he fell, then caught him once more with a crouching punch. Tetsuo struck him one last time with a low spin kick.

I backed Tetsuo away from Jack's body. Jack slowly regained his feet. In the dim light of the saloon, deep shadows pooled in the polygons of his round mask. If you looked at it just so, it almost seemed as though it was smiling.

Without taking a step toward Tetsuo, Jack spun into a roundhouse kick. The kick landed squarely on a nearby chair, sending it hurtling through the air. The flying chair struck Tetsuo dead-on.

Tetsuo reeled. He hadn't taken any damage, but being knocked off balance was bad enough. The outcome of the fight hinged on that moment. I shook the stick rapidly right to left. Tetsuo regained his balance just as another chair came flying. Son of a bitch. Reeling, Tetsuo turned toward the wall and retreated as Jack closed in and delivered an open-palmed thrust.

The counterhit sound FX played.

Tetsuo's body sailed into the air. Jack punched at his flying body. He canceled, then punched again. Tetsuo's body crashed into the wall. Jack caught him with an open-palmed thrust as he rebounded off the wall, and then he speed-dashed. Canceling, he punched once, then twice. He finished with a sweeping roundhouse kick.

Tetsuo's health gauge had fallen by nearly half.

I had no idea how familiar Jack's player was with the interior of the JTS Saloon. He might have known it even better than me. Whatever the case, he knew it well enough to come back with that chair trick after losing his balance on the table. He didn't disappoint. A tremor of excitement ran down my arms to my hands, shaking the stick clutched between my fingers. The mechanical sensors dutifully picked up the motion and converted it into neat packets of data to be sent down the fiber optic pipe running beneath the street. Not knowing the thrill I felt, Jack would interpret the motion no differently than any other.

That was the nature of the beast. The lines of communication available to us were gossamer-thin.

Jack closed in on Tetsuo's fallen body and timed a low spin kick to coincide with his rising off the ground. I dodged the attack with some quick stick work and sent Tetsuo underneath the swinging doors and out into the street with a crouching back dash.

Tetsuo was almost out of health. The next hit he took would be the last.

Jack came flying out of the saloon. I maneuvered Tetsuo around one of the columns, baiting him to follow me. He bit. Tetsuo held him in check with his fastest punch and retreated with a crouching back dash, stopping in the hollow beside the column. If Jack came at him with a high or low attack, they'd sail right over Tetsuo's head. I'd have a chance to score the counter I needed to pull this fight out. What's more, the incline would make it impossible to be thrown. It was the exact trick Ricky had pulled on Tetsuo.

My fingers tensed in anticipation.

Jack's response was unerring; he was a god in Sanchōme. I watched as he jumped into the air.

Jack had made the only move that would nullify the advantage I'd gained from the uneven ground. As Jack rose in the air, he kicked down at Tetsuo. Tetsuo did a back roll to dodge the strike. Jack and Tetsuo had swapped places.

Jack turned his back to the wall of the saloon. Here he was at his best.

If I could hit him, his body would rebound off the wall and I'd have a field day of midair combos. I knew exactly how he used walls to his advantage, but I had no choice but to attack. I needed a combo that packed some major damage or I didn't stand a chance of turning this fight around.

Tetsuo threw a middle punch. Jack blocked. I chained a low spin kick onto a crouching punch, then canceled.

Jack turned and jumped. Tetsuo released a middle spin kick. Jack air-blocked, avoiding the potential counterhit, and then pushed off the wall to complete his triangle jump.

Now Jack was behind Tetsuo. He had used the same move in his fight against Keith.

If I canceled my kick and turned to face him, Jack would still beat Tetsuo to the attack. If I followed through with the kick, Jack's next hit would be a counter. Strategically the only thing to do was cancel the kick and speed-dash toward the wall, but it would only buy me a moment's reprieve. Jack only needed one crouching punch to finish Tetsuo off.

It was all or nothing.

But Jack didn't know how much health Tetsuo had left. He didn't know he had taken damage fighting Hashimoto. He wouldn't know that one crouching punch stood between him and victory.

I made up my mind. If Jack was only going to throw rock and paper, it was time to bring scissors back into the game. I opened my eyes wide and stared at the screen.

There it was, in the middle of the screen. A barrel. The same barrel Ricky had used as a makeshift wall to set up a midair combo on Tetsuo. Tetsuo had taken a lot of damage because of that barrel. The large polygons even made it look heavy.

I canceled my spin kick. Pivoting on one leg, Tetsuo spun around to deliver a reverse spin kick. Rotating as he slid down the edge of the depression, he caught the barrel with the tip of his toes.

Under the full force of his kick, the barrel began to roll. The impact pushed Tetsuo back by a handful of pixels. Jack's punch missed.

Unfazed, Jack continued his attack. The kick he had chained onto the punch came within inches of Tetsuo's back. Then the barrel hit.

Jack's body flew up over the barrel, rising slightly into the air.

The whole thing had taken less than a second.

When a split second stands between you and life or death, you don't have time to think before you react. Your fingers do what they've been trained to do. *They* give the commands. From there on out, I was on autopilot.

Tetsuo caught the flying body with his fastest punch. I canceled and threw another punch, then a flying knee. Jack's body hit the barrel again. I punched him as he bounced off a second time. Canceling the kick I chained onto the punch, I tacked on a heel drop. Jack's body struck the ground. I caught him with a crouching punch as he bounced off the ground and then darted forward with a buffered speed dash. I canceled and threw a standing low spin kick. Another speed dash and I drove a fist down hard into his body.

Jack had stopped moving. A moment later, he vanished without a sound.

Tetsuo stood alone in the street.

I stared at my twenty-five-inch TV. It was only when I heard the AFK chime warning me I'd been inactive that I realized I'd won.

A HOT WIND pushed dry air through Shinjuku. Two straight days of rain had washed away the smog, leaving a turquoise blue sky outside the window. I picked a butter roll cloud out of the pack drifting slowly over the city. The hint of a smile spread across my face.

It was 8:55 AM. I was in my logic class, seventh row from the front. It was the last lecture of the semester, but apparently that wasn't enough to keep Uemura the Elder from attacking the chalkboard with a vengeance. Muttering complaints about the heat under his breath, he flew across the board even faster than usual. I was already on my third sheet of loose-leaf paper. My right hand had gone completely numb.

"This seat taken?"

I lifted my head at the sound of Fumiko's anime-saccharine voice. Without a word, I moved the bag I'd used to save her spot out of the seat next to me.

Fumiko sat down and started unpacking her bag, which was easily three times as thick as mine. She took her 0.7 mm mechanical pencil and silver-rimmed glasses from their respective cases. Her name was written on the front of her college-ruled notebook in letter-perfect characters.

I pushed my notes and a blue attendance card to her with a flourish. It was the last spare blue card I had, but it didn't matter.

"Your handwriting's terrible." Fumiko peered suspiciously at my notes through the thick lenses of her glasses.

"Sorry."

"I can't even read half of it."

"I can."

"If you're the only person who can read it, it's not writing. It's code."

Fumiko insisted that notes you couldn't read weren't any good. You couldn't count on remembering what you'd written, so you needed to write well enough that anyone could read them. I told her that with the amount of notes we had to take every week for Uemura the Elder, it didn't matter what condition they were in. She just smiled that hamburger-shop smile.

Fumiko fought back a yawn as she copied notes down off the board.

"Not getting much sleep?" I asked.

"Some."

"What have we here?"

"I was studying."

It took Fumiko five minutes to copy the notes I had spent half an hour transcribing, but her handwriting was still two hundred fifty-six times neater.

Uemura the Elder was humming along in front of the chalkboard. The morning light spilling into the room erupted into a halo as it struck the gel that had hardened in his hair. He definitely had his younger brother beat hands down in the hair department.

Looking back and forth from Fumiko's short bob to Uemura the Elder's neatly parted Carl Sagan coiffure, it occurred to me that given the choice between his associate professorship or a fine head of hair, Uemura the Younger would probably have chosen the hair.

That afternoon, Fumiko and I went into Shinjuku. She said she had some shopping to do. When I told her I'd seen *The Hustler*, she admitted to spending all day Sunday in an arcade. Apparently she dragged her brother out of bed to help her practice her combo moves in the neighborhood arcade. Last night she pulled an all-nighter reading a strategy guide.

I mussed Fumiko's hair. Maybe there was hope for her yet.

"Don't do this on my account."

Fumiko tugged hard at my shirttail. "Who said I was?"

"Why else would you?"

"I have my honor to defend."

"You gotta be good if you wanna defend anything."

"I'll get good, then."

"Won't be easy."

"We'll see."

Fumiko claimed to have lost the game I watched her play because she had chosen the wrong character. Apparently the karateka wasn't for her.

With an eagle claw, she swore she had the punch-cancel-palm thrust-cancel-palm thrust-punch-punch-cancel-chain low spin kick counter finishing move down cold. An E-rank combo that was a specialty of Tanaka's.

I looked up at the narrow strip of sky from the bottom of a canyon of skyscrapers. Before long she'd be better than Pak.

"Oh, one other thing I meant to ask, Eddie." Fumiko's smile gleamed with mischief. "You finally beat Minnesota Fats?"

"I dropped out of the tournament."

"For real?"

"For real."

"After you turned down my dinner invitation?"

"I ran into someone I'd been trying to find for a long time."

"Who? A girl?"

"I don't know."

"How can you not know?" I must have laughed then. "I saw that. Come on, let's hear it."

"I really don't know. You just have to take my word."

"Lies!"

"It's true. And quit pulling my shirt!"

I told Fumiko all about *Versus Town* then.

Tetsuo and his school uniform and wooden clogs. Hashimoto the ninja. Ben the bartender. Ricky the asshole. The maternal Masumi. The JTS Saloon tucked away in the warrens of Sanchōme. I told Fumiko the whole tale of the make-believe city and the make-believe character named Jack.

I told her why I wanted to become the best. Why I practiced combo moves on wooden dummies. Why I chose to fight Jack instead of Pak. And she listened to every word.

When Masumi and Hashimoto came to the saloon after the fight, I told them I had beaten Jack. Masumi emoted a toast to my success with a glass of whiskey and water. Hashimoto only stood there in his tuxedo and shrugged.

And that was the end of it. Tonight, somewhere far to the north, Hashimoto would be planning his next investigation even as the usual suspects filed into JTS. Life in Versus Town would go on as it always had.

The only thing that had changed was Ganker Jack. I didn't expect Tetsuo to ever see him again in the virtual world any more than I expected to see Lui again in the real one.

The place Jack and Tetsuo fought only existed online in a make-believe city, and it only existed while we were there, locked in a battle only we knew. That place was mine as much as it was Jack's. I earned it when I beat him, and he earned it when he lost. That was why we could never meet again. And even if we did, that one shining moment that existed between us was gone. It existed somewhere beyond our reach.

Now Fumiko and I were free to search for our own place, our own shining moment. Not my search for Jack, or Fumiko's search for the blue cat. I was ready and willing, if she was.

I turned to her as we walked. "Wanna catch a movie?"

"Nope. Today we're shopping."

"Again?"

"Is that a complaint?"

"A complaint? From me? No, I didn't hear any complaint."

"I'm pretty sure that was a complaint."

I took Fumiko's tiny hand in my own. The smells of a new summer surrounded us as we walked side by side through Shinjuku.

With Jack out of the way, I had decided to give Tetsuo some

much-needed rest. So it was purely chance that we passed the
arcade on Kokusai-dōri, and mere coincidence that I happened
to spot Pak inside.

The head-to-head game cabinet had been moved near the
entrance. It would seem the arcade was holding an event to
allow any brave soul to try their hand against the winner of
the second season tournament.

A girl in a sailor uniform sat beside Pak. If I had to guess,
I'd say she was Keith. When Tetsuo failed to show up for his
semifinal match, Keith received the spot as runner-up in the
match he'd lost against Tetsuo. Keith had gone on to beat Tanaka
and advance to the finals.

Pak dispatched the nameless snake boxer to advance to the
finals where he beat Keith to win the tournament. He had honed
his sharp look, and his skills, to the point it could probably
slice through a butcher block.

Fumiko watched the monitor as he played. "He's pretty good."

"You could say that."

"You're better though, right?"

"I'm not sure."

"But you beat Jack. I thought Jack was the best there was."

"Not everybody would agree."

"I don't think I understand." Fumiko touched her finger to
my chin. There was mischief in her eyes. The faint, sweet smell
of olive trees tickled my nose. "You want to play him?"

"Not especially." I had learned to filter my thoughts.

Fumiko translated. "So you don't especially want to play
him, but deep down inside, you might be tempted."

"That's right."

"You can play him once, *if* you buy me dinner," Fumiko
purred.

"Expensive game."

"You owe me after I had to cancel your birthday dinner."

I folded my arms. "This Saturday. Ebisu."

"A deal's a deal. Have at it."

"You're a real slave driver."

I sat down opposite Pak and pressed the A Button.

With a *click* I was no longer Etsuro Sakagami. I had become a karateka.

That day, I didn't bother keeping track of how many games I won.

BONUS ROUND

I PRESSED THE Ⓐ **BUTTON** and was no longer Jun Yamanouchi.

I had become Hashimoto.

My thumb worked the directional pad. Familiar music played through my headphones. The lights in my room were off. The storm shutters on the window were closed—I had taped cardboard over them to cover the gaps between the slats. My alarm clock was moping in the corner, collecting dust. It had made audible *ticks* as it counted away the seconds, but that was before I had torn out the batteries. The only source of light in the room was my flat-screen monitor; it cast a pale glow on the game console and my hands gripping the controller.

The nights are quiet in Otaru. The noise from my parents' television downstairs vibrated up through the floor. I could feel it in my ribs. My body lay half on my futon, my torso propped up on my elbows. But my mind was already wandering the streets of Versus Town.

Sanchōme was filled with the same old digital sounds under the same old turquoise blue sky. It was just past eleven o'clock at night. I spotted some familiar characters moving across the twenty-four-inch screen.

It'd been three months since Pak's win in the second season tournament.

No one had seen Jack. The Ganker of Sanchōme was gone. But the JTS Saloon was the same as ever. Right where it always had been. Most of the faces there were the same too: Hashimoto, Masumi, Ben, and Ricky. Seemed like RL had gotten its claws into Tetsuo's player though. Sometimes he'd be there when I logged in, and sometimes he wouldn't. When I did run into him, he'd often just be pacing back and forth along the streets of Sanchōme, like a lion in a cage.

Ninja Hashimoto was currently on the trail of another mystery—the biggest since Ganker Jack in fact.

The caper was a theft in RL: the mysterious disappearance of Pak's tournament trophy last week. The trophy itself wasn't particularly valuable. From the pictures I'd seen on the net, it looked pretty cheap. Not the kind of thing you could get much money for.

Pak's player had been at an arcade event when it happened. He'd only taken his eyes off of it for a second. Just long enough for the trophy to be stolen.

This intrigued me. Here we had something of extremely little value being stolen in plain sight in a crowded, public place. A trophy like that is valuable only because of the achievement it represents. It doesn't work the other way around. No pawnshop would ever take it, and you couldn't put it on your shelf and expect anyone to praise you for it. It wasn't impressive to *have* the trophy—it was impressive to *be* the player who won it.

Versus Town Networks, Inc., the game's owner, had put up an announcement on its homepage asking for the trophy's return, no questions asked. The public forums were up in arms and even the polygons of Sanchōme looked a little jumpy, as though they were afraid something might come along and steal *them*.

I pride myself on being in the know, and investigating this kind of thing was Hashimoto's raison d'être, so how could I resist looking into it? Here in Versus Town, the only real "meaning" came from a push of the directional pad. To get any more involved, the player had to put a part of themselves into the game. But that was like throwing dry ice in a bucket to make fog. Stop adding ice, and it all fades away. That was why Tetsuo's player wasn't logging in much these days. Jack had been his dry ice, but now that the saga of Tetsuo and Jack was over, he had no reason left to come to Versus Town. That was the nature of the game—and if you have something worth doing in RL, more power to you, I say.

As for me, I have nothing but the game. I got accepted to university in Tokyo only to run screaming three months later. Now I'm a professional shut-in. Who better to poke around the Internet trying to discover why someone would risk so much to steal something worth so little?

When I first retreated into my apartment down in Tokyo, I had this crazy idea that if I just went home the smell of the air would cure me. I'd be a regular person again. But when they finally dragged me back, I found that somehow the hands on my internal clock were moving at a different speed than those of my high school friends. We were off by about five seconds every hour or something. I couldn't input the correct commands to communicate with them anymore; the timing was all off. So I resumed the life I had taken up so briefly in Tokyo and shut myself away in my room to play games. *What if*, I wondered, *I'm at the cutting edge of human evolution?* Maybe my brain is more highly evolved. It's the kind of thing that, a century ago, only the nobility or the particularly well off would have even dreamed of contemplating. What would a lounging Roman aristocrat think if they saw how I was living? They'd probably think I had it all. "What a life," they'd say. Or not. Whatever.

Of course my parents were worried about me. Then again, sometimes I caught them actually being happy about their own son quitting school and coming back home, which only served to reinforce my notions about the stupidity of parents. In any case, stupidity is what let me spend my days playing games, so I couldn't complain.

I mashed the directional pad, sending Hashimoto running toward Sanchōme. I didn't take any shortcuts, choosing instead the streets where I knew I'd run into a lot of other characters. Even after the text bubbles had faded over the heads of people talking in the street, I could read what they had been saying in my log. I could analyze it later to check for any chatter about the case. If you put together the right team, you could track just about every conversation taking place in Versus Town.

Hashimoto made his way to JTS. Just inside an alleyway, I saw someone on the screen—a man, wearing a school uniform one size too small. Or maybe he was just one size too big. He wore big wooden sandals on his feet. His hair was all spiked, like the protagonist in a manga, and he wore a white headband. It was the karateka Tetsuo, toughest fighter in Sanchōme, a virtual city block brimming with fighters.

I pulled out my keyboard and started typing in a greeting. A text bubble appeared over Hashimoto's head.

> Tetsuo. It has been too long.
> About a week, right? I've been busy.
> Be warned: the way of the housewife with too much time on her hands is a dangerous path.
> Me? A housewife? Hardly.
> It was merely a jest.

I entered a command and Hashimoto nodded knowingly.

I could see Tetsuo was his usual new self: a stressed-out carnivore. Though his texture-mapped face hadn't changed one pixel, he was moving *listlessly*. Or maybe it was just that Tetsuo's player's clock and the clock of this virtual city weren't quite in sync.

Tetsuo spoke.

> Okay, to tell the truth, I got this problem IRL. Thought I'd head down to JTS and talk to the guys there about it.
> No good ever comes of bringing RL problems here, friend.
> Oh, I know that. It's just not the kind of thing I can talk to anyone in RL about.
> It is the way of things to discuss RL problems with RL people, is it not? Have you no friends in whom you might confide?

Tetsuo seemed to think for moment.

> There were some guys in middle school and high school I used to think were friends. But we've grown apart since entering university. I guess I have one friend I could tell, but I haven't talked to her in months. She might not even be around anymore.

> A sadder tale I have not heard for some time.

> It's different with you?

> There are those whom my player considers to be friends. However, whether or not they consider my player to be a friend is unknown.

> No surprise there.

Tetsuo flung up his arms on-screen. In a place like the net, where a new hero was born every day, it was sad to think that this foundering, lost fellow was the man who rubbed Ganker Jack's face in the dirt and got away with it. I knew I should have let it rest, but my fingers moved of their own accord.

> Tell me, Tetsuo. What troubles you?

Tetsuo didn't move. After a few moments, words began to fill the bubble hanging over his head.

> You hear about Pak's tournament trophy getting stolen?

> How could anyone who has been in Versus Town over the last week not have heard?

> Great. Figures.

> This is what concerns you? I fail to see how Pak losing his trophy would affect you in any way.

> It wouldn't if it were only missing.

> I am afraid you've lost me. What possible connection could there be between Pak's loss and your distress?

> Look, first I need you to promise me you won't tell anyone.

> A ninja says nothing.

> I mean it.
> …
> Very funny.
> I promise you I will speak of this to no one.

The moment the words appeared on-screen over Hashimoto's head, Tetsuo quickly forward-dashed from one end of the narrow alleyway in which we stood down to the other and back—checking to see if any other characters were close enough to eavesdrop on our conversation.

> This is quite the build-up.

Tetsuo approached and addressed Hashimoto again. His features betrayed nothing. Characters in *Versus Town* showed no sadness, joy, anger…or fear.

> Just between you and me, I know where Pak's trophy is.
> This is most unexpected news! Though I cannot see why you would wish to conceal it. You should tell everyone as quickly as possible.
> Can't do that.
> Why not?
> Because it's at my house.

For a second, I stared at the words on the screen, not comprehending. Hashimoto, in full ninja garb, stood there on the screen like a lifeless puppet. It wasn't until Tetsuo started typing again that my brain finally grasped what he was telling me.

> Someone sent it to me. Out of the blue. I don't even know who it was.

In some ways, I had always thought of Tetsuo as Hashimoto's

shadow. Or perhaps you might call him another possible Hashimoto, the path not chosen. The path that Tetsuo's player *hadn't* chosen in RL was the path on which I found myself. Somewhere back in the endlessly branching tree of possible paths, he had taken one path, while I stood mired in the same spot at the fork in the road, unable to follow. In this way, I felt we were connected.

In RL, Jun Yamanouchi was his parents' only son. I had a birth certificate and even health insurance. But from the viewpoint of productive society, I might as well have not existed. All this made me feel that as Hashimoto I should take this opportunity to help the character Tetsuo. Though one might consider it ironic for a person left stranded at the crossroads of life to lend aid to one who had already passed beyond him, it occurred to me that maybe this sort of thing actually happened all the time.

I found myself chuckling. The chuckle transmitted itself down my arm into the directional pad, and, without warning, Hashimoto executed a perfect somersault on the screen.

Tetsuo seemed surprised.

> What was that for?
> Alas, my hand merely slipped. Tetsuo, your concern is now my concern. Have no fear. All will be resolved.

TETSUO OFFERED ME HIS RL PHONE NUMBER, but I refused and began my own investigation. Tetsuo was a bit dubious about my prospects, but I had already decided to see this through Hashimoto's way. No good would come of intruding too far upon another player's RL existence—or from another player intruding upon mine. In Versus Town I was only Hashimoto, and Tetsuo was Tetsuo, and that was the way it should be.

Also, it occurred to me that if the trophy thief had been able to uncover Tetsuo's player's RL address, then it couldn't be all that difficult for me to do should the need arise. Tetsuo's player hadn't been so rash as to post his address online, but someone at Versus Town Networks, Inc., would certainly have access to it, and a simple scan of our conversation logs would shed some light on where he lived. From our limited conversations, I already knew that he was a university student with too much time on his hands. Of course, there was also a possibility that the thief was someone already known to him—maybe even someone who lived next door—who just happened to be a resident of Versus Town as well.

The question I needed to grapple with first was not the thief's identity, but why they would bother sending the trophy to Tetsuo's player. I did not think it was an entirely meaningless act. Nor would all this end were he to simply return the trophy to Pak.

The most obvious reason I could think of was that someone with an axe to grind with Tetsuo was trying to frame him. But if that were the case, I would have expected the thief to be spreading rumors already. I had checked my logs and no one suspected Tetsuo of any wrongdoing. So that line of reasoning was probably a dead end. I crossed it off my mental checklist.

Just about anyone who had spent time in Sanchōme knew that Tetsuo had defeated Ganker Jack. That didn't necessarily make him the toughest guy in Versus Town, though some might credit him with that title anyway. Others held that only the top-ranked player in the tournament was the best. Maybe it was this odd disparity of opinion that had inspired our thief to take action. Maybe he (or she) was trying to start a fight between the two champs of *VT*.

I waded through the sea of information, a can of cola (bought for me by my parents) in one hand. Many people seem to think that shut-ins sit around eating pizza all day, but that couldn't be further from the truth. Appetite is a sign that one still possesses RL aspirations. A true shut-in never exercises, so hunger is never really a problem. Their muscles atrophy, they grown thin. I rarely eat at all. The only thing accumulating inside me was the information that came rolling in from the net like waves from the sea.

I decided to start by making contact with those who had joined in the hunt for Jack, and then looked into finding out more about this *Versus Town* arcade event. At the same time, I began my analysis of my conversation log, focusing on tournament contestants and Sanchōme residents. First I sorted their conversations by category. Then I divided the conversations by player name and ran searches for keywords. Finally I looked at connections with other characters based on those words and plotted all the connections on a grid. It might have seemed like a fairly elaborate process, but with the help of some freeware applications off the net, I hardly had to do a thing.

At the center of my grid was, of course, Pak. Next to him was Tetsuo. Everyone around them had ranked highly in the second season tournament. Tanaka—by all accounts a jock—and the nameless snake boxer were way off to one edge of the grid. But there was another person near the middle, forming a triangle with Tetsuo and Pak: the snake boxer Ricky. Not a weak fighter by any means, but not the strongest combatant.

Though it made perfect sense for Ricky—whose devotion to Pak and open dislike of Tetsuo were both well known—to be at the center of the rumors circulating about the trophy snatching, something about it didn't quite fit. That Ricky was despicable was a fact. But trying to frame Tetsuo's player just didn't fit with what Hashimoto knew of Ricky's free-form fighting style. Freestyle fighting still means fighting by the rules. And theft was certainly not in the rules. Maybe it made more sense to suspect someone far from the center of the grid. The real thief might have taken steps to avoid any rumors. And I had to admit the possibility that Tetsuo's player was simply pulling my leg. Maybe he had even stolen the trophy himself.

"Anyone can come up with theories. What you need is a plan."

No wiser words have ever been spoken—of that I have no doubt. And that's not a quote from some historic figure or famous scholar. The lead character in a manga I once read had said it.

As long as you're online, it's easy to find a solution to just about any of life's little problems. Dr. Google had a way of coming up with answers for every question. The real impediment to solving a problem was *understanding* what you learned from the Internet, then putting it into practice. You might know the commands for a killer move, but if your fingers can't convert knowledge to action you'd never win a match. It was the same thing in RL, and though we might have the knowledge we need to solve a real world problem, it's never easy to know how to act and when. This little incident that had occurred in the narrow space between *Versus Town* and RL was going to be one of those kinds of problems, I could tell.

For the time being, I decided to narrow my investigation

to Ricky, Tanaka, and the nameless snake boxer. In the case of Ricky, a regular at the JTS Saloon, I would have Masumi collect log data for me. Unfortunately, because of my promise to Tetsuo, I couldn't enlist all the people I would've liked to for a real sea-of-people web crawler strategy. Instead, I sent Hashimoto to the arena in Nichōme on his own.

The arena was the center of Versus Town. A recent server-side upgrade had made a new combo attack possible, and the place was packed with people logged in from all over the country to try it out. It had recently become fashionable to use a skinning mod to make one's character look like some character from a manga or anime. I spotted several people in a group who all looked like this chick from a late-night anime I'd seen once. That is, their faces all looked like hers, but their bodies were those of their original characters. They were in a circle, trying out new moves. I could hear the smacking sound FX of successful counters all around, making the place sound like a concert where the orchestra was made up entirely of bass drums and cymbals.

It would be enough to linger by one wall in order to gather log data. I decided to go in undercover, changing Hashimoto's clothes to those worn by that same late-night anime chick. His face I left the same, which probably had the opposite effect of attracting more attention.

Just past four AM, when most of the place was full of characters standing idle after their players had dozed off or gone AFK, someone approached Hashimoto.

> Nice face. lol
> Alas, I could not bring myself to disguise my trademark features.
> I'm totally screen-capping this.
> Please! No likenesses of my face!
> But, dude, it's so funny!

My assailant was also wearing a late-night anime costume, with a long staff strapped uselessly to his back. I recognized him as one of the people who had helped in the hunt for Jack. I had no idea who the player was. Turning to him, I typed:

> Though I realize it may not appear so, I am, in fact, undercover on an investigation. What is it you want of me?
> I just wanted to tell you that I figured it out.
> Figured what out?
> That thing you were asking about. lol. You know, that arcade thing?
> Do tell.
> A month ago there was this local tournament at an arcade in Sugamo. Well, one of the guys who works there happens to be a friend of mine, and he's not the brightest kid on the block when it comes to information control. Turns out he left a notebook with the addresses of all the contestants out on a counter. lol! Talk about epic fail.
> Who were the contestants?
> Well, the winner was a karateka, most likely Tetsuo's player. Second place was this elementary school kid playing a snake boxer. People were saying it was Jack.
> The style of snake boxer who came in a strong fourth in the tournament resembles that of Jack.
> Well, yeah, there's no way to be sure who's who. But some people were saying that Ricky's player and Tanaka's player were there too.
> More and more intriguing.
> Totally. So what's all this got to do with the missing trophy?
> Sorry, but I am not yet at liberty to say.
> lol. Stingy-ass.

That some confidential information had slipped out into the open was no surprise. The players of *Versus Town* were simply average people who happen to be very good at fighting games, not Cyber Czars obsessed with data security. However, my informant's story had revealed to me the fascinating fact that everyone I had considered up until now in my investigation had likely been together in one place, and any one of them could have had access to Tetsuo's address. Judging from what I knew of Tetsuo's player, he wasn't the sort to announce who he was to the crowd, but a powerful combatant such as he would reveal himself before long through his game play. Someone could have identified him and made their move.

> I upped a picture I took of the notebook with my cell phone to the usual spot. It's got personal info all over it, so erase it once you've DL'd, k?

> I thank you. I promise that once my investigation is complete, I will tell you all I am able to, so long as it does not infringe upon anyone else's privacy.

> You'd better for all the help I've given you. lol

The anime chick walked away.

The players in this grand scheme were all coming together. Still, I had no idea who had done it or why. I sat there awhile turning it over in my head, when I noticed sunlight spilling in from behind the cardboard on the window. I took a sip of warm cola. The early morning arena was empty. The back of my eyes burned. I logged out and went to the kitchen downstairs to get something to eat.

As I sat at the table in the gradually brightening room, eating for breakfast what my mom had left me for dinner, I surfed the net on my laptop. The morning sun was gleaming brightly off the neighbor's roof. The blue tiles shimmered, making it hard to read the screen. The light at this time of day always depressed me.

"Hey, you're up." The living room door opened. My mother was standing there, looking at me in surprise. "Morning, Jun.

Didn't expect to find you here this early."

I drained a cup of reheated soup and didn't answer. My mother didn't seem to mind. She stomped back into the living room and opened the windows, then the storm shutters, letting in fresh air along with a ray of sunlight that stabbed the dim room like a sword. The screen was all but illegible now.

"My, they're early this year," my mother said.

I looked around and saw something brown moving on the single tree behind our house. The tree was a thin-limbed chestnut growing on the tiny patch of ground next to a storage shed. I suspected it was malnourished because it never grew any bigger, and it certainly never produced any chestnuts. A bird that looked something like an obese sparrow sat on one of the branches and failed to hide beneath a freshly sprouted leaf. The bird shifted on its perch, trying to avoid the combo attack of the branches and the thorny leaves around it.

"That a sparrow?"

"No, silly. It's a thrush."

My mother laughed. The thrush launched from its perch, disappearing into the sky over the waking town. It had all happened in a matter of seconds. I turned my attention back to the screen.

I downloaded the image of the address book and passed my eyes over it. In all honesty, I couldn't care less about Tetsuo's player. What interested me was this situation where several other players had access to his address. The information trickled slowly through my sleep-deprived head. But when I saw the name of the one man registered as a karateka, I nearly fell out of my seat. It was the name of the only friend I had made during my few months at university.

CHAPTER 3

IT WAS STRANGE reuniting online with someone from RL.

Etsuro Sakagami—the one friend I had made at university. I had no delusions that our friendship had been anything but one-sided. He had kept on keeping on as a student after I'd flown the coop, after all, and from Tetsuo's conversational logs it looked like while I'd been frozen in time up in Hokkaido he'd gotten himself a girlfriend. It would be arrogant to assume he was even the same person anymore.

To be perfectly honest, I was a little envious.

Here was a guy who had made it both in the virtual world of *Versus Town*, with his victory over Ganker Jack, and in the real world at the *same time*. It almost seemed unfair for someone who still maintained ties to RL to have a trophy like Jack on his shelf.

Life isn't fair. My parents' words. The words of every parent in the world.

I knew that. I also knew that Tetsuo had been the perfect fighter to take down Jack. He was the kind of guy capable of abandoning the arena in favor of settling things on the streets of Sanchōme. What would it have meant if Hashimoto had done the honors? Little, probably. Still, I couldn't help but feel that Tetsuo's actions had a concrete meaning, while Hashimoto's drifted like mist, indiscriminate and unfathomable, even to me.

I had remained standing still while the distance between us grew. The same distance that had been growing between me and an indeterminate number of people in RL, of course, but now that I knew Tetsuo was Etsuro I couldn't help but compare my lack of progress specifically with his successes.

I had gone home and he had *let* me. What would have happened had he extended a friendly hand at just the right moment? Nothing, I knew. Everything that had happened to me in RL was my fault. My problems were mine to solve, not his—which begged the question: why help him now?

I returned to my room—ignoring my mother's editorial comments behind me—and once again entered the online world of Sanchōme, a ghost town in these early morning hours. I moved Hashimoto mechanically down the streets, checking each structure in turn as though I might find something hidden within their pixels.

I looked up the thrush we had seen—a dusky thrush, apparently—and determined it was indeed a different bird from a sparrow. According to Wikipedia, the dusky thrush rarely sings. A private bird, it preferred to lurk in the shade of the undergrowth. I could identify with that.

I don't know how far separated Etsuro and Tetsuo were in Etsuro's mind, but in my own mind there was a clear division between Hashimoto the character and me the player. It was Hashimoto who heard Tetsuo's request, Hashimoto who was doing Tetsuo a favor. It had nothing to do with either me or Etsuro Sakagami. That was the theory, but putting it into practice was another matter. Everything about my current task felt onerous. I couldn't think clearly and often wished the whole thing would just melt away like an ice sculpture set outside on a summer day. How much easier that would be.

I opened a door to a house of stacked polygons, went in for a look around, and then moved on to the next. There was no indication of night or day in my room. The cardboard strip on the shutters was firmly in place, and the clock still sat silent, its batteries removed. The cola I'd taken from the fridge the night before had gone from winter cold to the lingering chill of an autumn day. On screen, the Versus Town sky was the same turquoise blue it always was.

I was on my twentieth or thirtieth house when I saw a face

through one of the semi-translucent windows—someone standing on the road outside. If my memory served, it looked exactly like Ganker Jack.

Jack? He shouldn't be here anymore. The man had practically been looking for someone to bury him. Why would he ever come back? Had he heard about Tetsuo's slow withdrawal from the game? Or maybe Jack's player had stolen the trophy. If that were the case, I would have to rebuild my entire set of working assumptions.

My head moved sluggishly, but my fingers launched into precise action. Hashimoto dashed forward, leaping over a sofa, kicked open the door, and ran in the direction of the mysterious character.

Jack was a middleweight, Hashimoto a lightweight. I would have no trouble catching up. I had my laptop open and had been intending to check some data, but there was no time for that now. The slightest blink of delay in entering a command could decide everything. Luckily, I knew this place better than the back of my hand. As long as I didn't get into any fights, nothing could slow me down.

As I ran, Hashimoto leveraged a small jump onto a hedgerow into a large jump. I looked around in midair and found the person I was looking for. It was Jack's face, all right. But the body was wrong—it looked like the girl from that late-night anime everyone seemed to be copying lately.

My mark ducked into an alley. I mashed some commands and sent Hashimoto in after him. There he was. I stopped Hashimoto about three and a half steps away—just out of dash-throw range.

> Who are you?

Without answering, my mark lifted his girlish arms and removed the mask, which should have been impossible. Masks in *Versus Town* weren't placed on the face, they were directly applied to facial textures. If there had been a patch to change this, I hadn't heard anything about it.

My surprise at that was nothing compared to what I saw next. I was looking at myself—Hashimoto, to be precise. My mark wore the face of a grumpy old man on the body of an anime girl.

> I will ask you again. Who are you?

A speech bubble appeared above the mystery figure's head, his diction mimicking my own antiquated style.

> Before I may respond to your request, I have a question of mine own. I want to hear your thoughts on the meaning of our existence here in Versus Town.

Was he serious or merely having a laugh at my expense? I had no way to tell. What seemed clear was that he had looked into the window of the house with the express purpose of drawing me out. I was the mark, not him. There was nothing to lose and everything to gain by taking this matter very seriously indeed. Leaving my controller where I could grab it at a moment's notice, I began to type.

> While performing a hundred push-ups might make one's arms strong, vaulting an E-rank wall one hundred times does not make one any stronger. All that we can advance is our sense of arcane command timings, all of which could change with the next patch. In other words, all characters in *Versus Town* stand upon the deck of a ship that might capsize at any moment.

> Not what I would have expected to hear from Hashimoto's player. Why, your assessment of *VT* is practically the same as that of the sneering old man who dismisses all this as a "virtual" waste of time.

The impostor Hashimoto looked as unimpressed as an impassive mask of polygons could look.

> Then what would you say we are?
> Focusing prisms. The online environment possesses the capacity to augment one or more parts of a player's personality. The imaginary character we create online is a delusion or fantasy, if you prefer, above and beyond the fantasies we carry around with us in RL.
> We're just fantasies, then?
> We cling to fantasies in both the real and virtual. What I wish to point out is that those fantasies are different.

What this Hashimoto was saying was perfectly in character for Hashimoto. I felt almost like he'd stolen Hashimoto away from me, leaving me, the player, standing naked in an alley in Versus Town. Not a pleasant sensation.

> So what are you trying to

I began to type, but the other Hashimoto cut me off with a stream of text in his own speech bubble.

> The real Etsuro Sakagami would never turn to Jun Yamanouchi for help unraveling a mystery. Why? Because the real Jun Yamanouchi doesn't match the RL image of someone capable of unraveling mysteries—he doesn't fit the fantasy. Not so with the imaginary online character Hashimoto. He might be capable where Jun Yamanouchi is not. At least, that's what Etsuro Sakagami thinks. He entrusts Hashimoto with a task he would never entrust to his player.
> Yes, but Hashimoto is merely a part of Jun Yamanouchi, a character whom I role-play, nothing more. How could Hashimoto divine anything I could not?

He spoke again.

> Of course the intellectual limitations of the player are those of the character. My brain and yours are the same, after all. Yet I, who possess augmented capacity for thought in a certain direction, have abandoned whole categories of things that you do, allowing you to choose from certain paths of action that you have already discarded because you did not require them. That is how I am able to arrive at conclusions well outside Jun Yamanouchi's usual framework of thought.

Apparently, the Hashimoto I was talking to was the real Hashimoto. He was making me feel like an impostor.

> Sounds like you already know the answer then.
> Of course I do. It's quite simple.
> Easy for me to say.
> It's not only a question of virtual theory. If you are able to leverage this new personality you have found within yourself, to accept it as part of your total being, then you can bring it back to serve the needs of Jun Yamanouchi in RL.
> Sounds complicated.
> I never said it would be easy.

Hashimoto deftly shrugged the polygons in his shoulders—one of my favorite emotes.

Back when all Sanchōme had been abuzz with talk of the ganker, Tetsuo hadn't been the only one hot on Jack's trail. There were plenty of guys out there looking to bring Jack down and make a name for themselves in the process, Hashimoto being one of them. But though I had been chasing Jack, I never wanted to defeat him. I couldn't claim the online miracle that was Jack all for myself. I wasn't so arrogant as to deprive all those people chasing after a fantasy of their one chance of justifying hours spent idly wandering the streets of Sanchōme just to satisfy my own sense of purpose.

Nor was there any guarantee that Hashimoto could have taken Jack down even had he gone that route. Rather, it was highly unlikely. That it seemed likely now was an illusion brought about because Tetsuo had defeated him and taken the title of reigning champion for his own. If I rewound my memory to the time before Tetsuo's victory, I found Jack standing like a monument over Versus Town: undefeatable, superhuman. For Tetsuo's player, Etsuro Sakagami, the decision to take on Jack couldn't have been an easy one. But he had chosen it and had made it across the tightrope to victory.

It had been an unusual situation, to say the least. They had decided to fight without an audience at all. That had been what Tetsuo wanted, of course. Jack as well, no doubt. Hashimoto himself understood the justice in it, and Pak hadn't seemed to mind either. But it must have been a particularly bitter ending—having been stuck lurking out of the spotlight—for whoever sent the trophy to Etsuro. That was why he was trying to reboot Jack's story now.

Hashimoto could simply walk away, and this second chapter in Jack's story would likely find its own ending, somewhere in between *VT* and RL. *But would it be an ending I wanted? No—it doesn't matter what I think.* Hashimoto, this imaginary character I had created, was me, but at the same time, not exactly "me." Hashimoto lacked some parts of my personality, while possessing others in even greater abundance than I did—probably a mixed blessing for him. For me, I had a little more flexibility. It all came down to whom I chose to favor at any given time: myself or Hashimoto.

I realized that it wasn't about whether I wanted a reboot of Jack's story. The question I really should be asking was, "Would Hashimoto want this new ending?" I could probably get through this as a bystander. That would be more my style anyway—to stand back, out of the action—especially now that I knew Tetsuo's player was my old friend. Yet the memory of my joy at having been, as Hashimoto, even a spectator at the miracle that was Ganker Jack and the frenzy that erupted around him pulled me irresistibly into the thick of it. I could not ignore that memory. To do so would be to allow RL to overwrite Hashimoto.

But would that be such a great loss? No matter how well I played the role of Hashimoto, I didn't really expect his character to rub off on me in any appreciable way. The potential for personal growth online was a fleeting thing, a little dream quickly lost in a deluge of data. Trying to catch it was akin to catching a silvery fish bare-handed.

Yet that hope for personal growth fueled my role-playing of Hashimoto. I had to conclude that it was vital to prevent RL considerations from destroying online potential, no matter how small that potential. The one who had stolen the trophy didn't understand this, and I couldn't abide that. It wasn't a question of who had been inconvenienced or who was helping whom. This was a personal affront to Hashimoto and every other resident of Versus Town. In a place where action was king, taking action *sans* understanding was the worst thing you could possibly do.

It fell to me to bury this second chapter before it even got started, and as Hashimoto I was uniquely qualified to do that. As a bystander, he had watched as Tetsuo pursued Jack. I was now quite sure that the trophy thief had also been one of Jack's pursuers. It would be a simple thing to simulate the thought patterns of someone who hadn't been happy to see things go the way they had.

I realized I'd been staring at my twenty-four-inch flat-screen monitor for some time without looking at anything in particular. The AFK chime in the game began to sound. In *Versus Town*, that warning only went off after several minutes of inactivity. I checked the time on my laptop and saw it was already ten PM in RL. I'd been dreaming.

Had I really been chatting with someone? Had I been playing

while I was asleep? It was possible that Jack's player had really shown up looking and acting like Hashimoto, and as long as he was acting like Hashimoto he would be Hashimoto. But why would Jack have any reason to go so far out of his way on my account? No, I must have been dreaming.

Real or not, the episode had left me with a new insight on the case. I now knew who the trophy thief was. Once I understood how he felt, it hadn't been hard. In fact, I realized the problem had never been the thief's identity. The real problem, one I still faced, was how virtual Hashimoto was going to get the drop on an RL thief.

CHAPTER 4

I PRESSED THE [A] BUTTON and became Ganker Jack.

Well, to be precise, I became Hashimoto, except today, Hashimoto was role-playing Jack. I looked just like him: a middleweight snake boxer. From the outside, it would have been impossible to tell the difference.

The time was nine PM. Still a little before peak time on the server. Hashimoto, in Jack-guise, stood in a relatively deserted Sanchōme. Tetsuo stood a short distance away, rotating his camera at regular intervals.

> You really think he'll bite?

Tetsuo asked. I entered my response.

> Absolutely.
> There isn't a single pixel moving around here besides us.
> Recall that I said it might take ten or even twenty attempts.
> Look, if you think you know who might have done it, why don't we just ask them?
> Knowing who stole the trophy in RL is immaterial. I know what I'm doing. Leave this to me.
> There you go again.
> Someone may be watching us. I suggest we speak no further.
> Fine, fine. Whatever you say.
> We should get started soon, with your leave. Same as before.

I did indeed have a pretty good idea of who the thief was, but there was a chance I had missed the mark. Still, I didn't really think that mattered. In this place where the only meaning lay in action, the thief's name was merely information. It was knowing *why* he had done what he had that was important.

This was the fifth such mock battle between Tetsuo and Hashimoto/Jack. I had already planted rumors in such a way that it would reach the ears of my suspect that Ganker Jack had returned. If my hypothesis was correct, a Jack reboot would be the one temptation the suspect could not resist.

I worked the controls, making Jack retreat back down a narrow alleyway. It was important that we always began our mock battles in precisely the correct predetermined locations.

> Let us begin.

I swapped controller plugs on the game console and pressed enter on my laptop. Jack sprang into action. When he had closed to three and a half steps, Tetsuo too began to move. Dodging Jack's opening kick by a hair, Tetsuo went on the offensive. Jack ran, Tetsuo in hot pursuit. A series of attacks and counters played out on my twenty-four-inch display, almost too fast for my eye to follow.

Obviously, I would never be able to control Jack as well as Jack's original player. Trying to pretend otherwise would only reveal me as an impostor to anyone with any combat experience, and my mark was one of the best fighters in Versus Town. So I had to improvise. Instead of controlling Jack's moves directly, I left that to a program on my laptop. Hashimoto-in-Jack-guise was free to engage in pitch-perfect choreographed combat against his sworn enemy.

Tetsuo dashed in close, grabbing Jack by the collar for a throw. Jack brushed Tetsuo's arms aside and the two of them rotated 45 degrees before separating again.

I could picture Etsuro Sakagami working his controller, far away, at the other end of a fiber optic cable in Saitama. Jack was merely playing out the predetermined steps in a solo dance, but with Tetsuo's accompaniment, the dance became a battle

royal. Tetsuo lunged and countered at preplanned intervals.
There was a margin of error of only a few seconds in the entire
fight. He truly was the best fighter in Sanchōme. I don't think
anyone else in the game could have pulled off such a perfectly
choreographed dance.

Jack and Tetsuo wore away at each other's defenses as their
fight slowly moved deeper and deeper into the backstreets of
Sanchōme.

Jack swept gracefully across the screen—a dance I could
no longer even pretend to be following. There was a different
personality within Hashimoto's body now. Now I was the
observer, watching him and Tetsuo spar. I had no idea what
Etsuro was feeling—only my laptop felt the force of his kicks
and quick jabs—but to me, it looked like a happy reunion of
two old friends trading blows beneath a clear blue sky.

The fight went on for ten minutes, when history was reversed
(for the fifth time) and Ganker Jack sealed his victory over
Tetsuo. Sprawled at Jack's feet, Tetsuo's body became translucent,
then faded entirely.

Our suspect was still a no-show. I yanked the USB cable out
of the console to replace the controller that would once again
put Jack under my control.

A bubble appeared in a corner of the screen.

> U Jack?

It took me three tries to get the controller plugged in. As I
was fumbling with the cable, another message appeared.

> R U Jack?

The controller clicked home. First I checked to make sure
that Hashimoto and the new arrival were three and a half steps
apart, then I began to type. From here on out, the fight would
be Hashimoto's. Tetsuo fought with the controller, Hashimoto

with the keyboard. And I couldn't leave this coming battle to my laptop bot.

> Regrettably, I am not.
> U beat Tetsuo.
> We were merely putting on a performance. I knew that if Tetsuo fought Jack, you would appear.

There was a pause before he replied.

> What?
> I am pleased to meet you. I am Hashimoto, gatherer of information various and sundry. It was you who sent Pak's trophy to Tetsuo, yes?
> U got proof?
> Plenty. You see, it was I who spread the rumor that Tetsuo and Jack would be fighting again, this time for possession of the trophy. Only one who knew that Tetsuo possessed the trophy in the first place would give the rumor any credence at all, i.e., you.

The man did not move.

He was a snake boxer, middleweight, wearing a nondescript martial arts uniform, with a nondescript texture on his face. It was exactly as I had predicted. This was the nameless snake boxer who had made top four in the second season tournament.

A moment passed before more text began to appear above the man's head.

> OK. What now?
> I would like you to answer some questions.
> OK.
> Why did you send the trophy to Tetsuo?

Neither the man nor Hashimoto moved a pixel. No one else

was in sight from where we stood. The only motion on the screen was the text scrolling above their heads.

> To give credit where it was due.
> But he DID receive due credit. I know of Tetsuo's strength. As do you, as did Jack. What other need could there possibly be?
> Everyone thinks Pak's number 1.
> Indeed, he is properly number one. He did win the tournament where such things are decided.
> Pak's a n00b!
> That has nothing to do with weakness or strength. That trophy was made to honor the one who took first place in the tournament. Not to honor the best fighter in Sanchōme. What Tetsuo deserves is a trophy for defeating Jack in a back alley.
> Like anyone would want that.
> In this town, there is no such thing as "money." There are no electricity bills, gas bills, water bills. There is nothing real here at all. The only thing that counts in Versus Town is action. All else, including titles and glory, eventually fades. Here, our actions are the only things that remain.

As I typed, the image of a saber-toothed tiger rose in my mind. Saber-toothed tigers were carnivores known to have existed in prehistoric times. The theory was that each generation of tiger had longer fangs than the previous, until they became too long and the species died out entirely. We here in Versus Town were much the same. This virtual place online would not exist forever. Its popularity would die out in half a year or so, and eventually the servers would shut down, leaving only a few memories and random data on a hard disk somewhere. This only made it all the more important that we make the most of our virtual selves—and our virtual fangs—while they lasted.

> Lol. What R U talking about? I have no idea.
> That is acceptable.

> So what? U want me to make an apology or something?
> There is no need.
> ???
> You need say nothing. I will have the trophy returned to
Pak. I will keep your identity a secret.
> How do I know you're telling the truth?
> Tetsuo asked me merely to solve the case, not find the thief.
> U going to protect me? Why?

I saw the snake boxer's body twitch. A stray finger on the
controller, perhaps.

> Consider it a consolation prize, for both of us.
> What? This is a prize? What does this have to do with
prizes?
> Everything.
> lol. What's that supposed to mean?

The nameless snake boxer was strong. If it was true that he
was still in elementary school, then in two or three years, he
might even be stronger than Tetsuo and Jack. But by trying
to tie a *Versus Town* fight to RL, he had proven himself an
unworthy opponent for Jack in the first place.

On one day, at one time, there had been a place within this
illusory town meant only for Jack's player and Etsuro Sakagami
to see. Hashimoto hadn't received a ticket to that show, sadly
enough. The key to solving the mystery of Jack had slipped from
my fingers at the last moment. I realized now why it had been
better that way. While there might have been some meaning
in the act of catching Jack, nothing would have come from it.
The miracle that Jack brought to Versus Town was meant only
to be shared with Tetsuo, and only once. I finally realized this.
Hashimoto's yearning for Jack had been one-sided.

Clearly this snake boxer had also been chasing after the Ganker.
No doubt it gave the Fates a good chuckle to bring the both of

us—two also-rans—together like this. Our meeting was like a bonus round in an epic battle, one which had meaning for only us. If Hashimoto was Tetsuo's shadow, then this snake boxer was Jack's. The snake boxer hadn't been fated to fight Jack, or even Tetsuo—he'd been fated to meet Hashimoto. Of course, it was probably only me who thought that. The snake boxer was almost certainly disappointed to find himself facing not the Ganker of Sanchōme returned, but a nosy rumor-mongering ninja.

I backspaced away what I had just typed, and instead I sent my usual catchphrase. It seemed to sum up how I was feeling nicely.

> It means I am ninja.
> Whatever, dude.
> Farewell.

As consolation prizes went, it wasn't bad. I would probably remember this meeting between me and the snake boxer for years to come. Maybe even for the rest of my life. It would please me if the snake boxer remembered it too, yet I had no guarantee he would. Perhaps this too was a one-sided affair, which would also be suitable for me, a shut-in playing a character who walked in the shadows of a virtual town.

~

> Thanks, man.

It was nine o'clock in the evening on the following day when I rejoined Tetsuo on a corner in Sanchōme. Tetsuo hadn't complained when I told him what had taken place, and he agreed to return the trophy to Pak...no return address. As I had been gearing myself up to persuade him, his nonchalant attitude was a bit of an anticlimax. Or perhaps it was just that he had nothing to say to Hashimoto and was simply happy to be done with the whole affair.

> Do not mention it. It was a simple task for one of my resources to accomplish.
> No, you really helped me out.
> I require no praise. Though I certainly don't mind it.
> Right, er, you're the best. Oh, that reminds me, there was something I wanted to ask you.
> What might that be? I regret I won't be able to supply you with so much as a hint regarding the identity of the thief.
> Not about that.
> What then?

Hashimoto put his hands at his hips. Tetsuo did not move. When I saw the next block of text displayed above his head, I had to blink twice before understanding it.

> Would you mind giving me your email address?
> Why would you need such a thing?
> I just thought it might be nice, now that we've met here and all.
> But I am Hashimoto, and you are Tetsuo. We need nothing else.
> I was afraid you'd say that.
> I have said it before.
> Well, you stick to your guns, I'll give you that.
> Our *Versus Town* characters are not us. They are an enhancement of parts of our personalities. Though we might become friends here, it is no guarantee we could be friends in RL. If you have time to be friends with my player, spend that time instead with your RL girlfriend, or other friends. Ah . . . you have no friends, right?
> I wouldn't say that.
> But you did say that before.
> Yeah, but when I started thinking about it, I realized I did have this one friend at university. Haven't seen him since he quit and went home, though. I'd still call him a friend—no

idea whether he'd say the same about me. Haven't talked to him in forever.

I lay half in my futon, hands trembling. I checked the screen. Hashimoto's face remained an impassive blank. I began to type, painstakingly, one letter at a time.

> Why would you still consider him a friend, then?
> Well, I don't know. I just thought about him recently because of all this. Made me want to talk to him again. Tell him about what had happened, you know?
> And you still consider this person a friend?
> Yeah, though like I said, it's probably pretty one-sided at this point.
> I would not be so sure.
> Well, maybe I'll try dropping him a line one of these days.
> I would think that most acceptable. I'd expect him to be pleased.
> Or maybe he's had it with Tokyo and would rather not be reminded I exist at all.
> I think not. Reach out, and you are sure to make contact.
> Heh. Then I suppose there is still a point to RL after all.
> Quite.

As I pressed the enter key, it occurred to me that save for *Versus Town* I had spent the last half-year doing absolutely nothing. If my friend were to suddenly call out of the blue, what would I talk with him about? I hadn't the faintest idea.

This would be a far more difficult problem for Hashimoto to solve than had been the mysterious misfortune that befell the karateka Tetsuo.

⌨ END

Photo by Yoshihiro Hagiwara

HIROSHI SAKURAZAKA

Born in 1970. After a career in information technology, he published his first novel, *Wizards' Web*, in 2003. His 2004 short story, "Saitama Chainsaw Massacre," won the 16th SF Magazine Reader's Award. His other novels include *All You Need Is KILL*, available from Haikasoru, and *Characters* (co-written with Hiroki Azuma).

HAIKASORU
THE FUTURE IS JAPANESE

THE NEXT CONTINENT BY ISSUI OGAWA

The year is 2025 and Otaba General Construction—a firm that has built structures to survive the Antarctic and the Sahara—has received its most daunting challenge yet. Sennosuke Touenji, the chairman of one of the world's largest leisure conglomerates, wants a moon base fit for civilian use, and he wants his granddaughter Taé to be his eyes and ears on the harsh lunar surface. Taé and Otaba engineer Aomine head to the moon where adventure, trouble, and perhaps romance await.

LOUPS-GAROUS BY NATSUHIKO KYOGOKU

In the near future, humans will communicate almost exclusively through online networks—face-to-face meetings are rare and the surveillance state nearly all-powerful. So when a serial killer starts slaughtering young people, the crackdown is harsh. And despite all the safeguards, the killer's latest victim turns out to have been in contact with three young girls; Mio Tsuzuki, a certified prodigy; Hazuki Makino, a quiet but opinionated classmate; and Ayumi Kono, her best friend. As the girls get caught up in trying to find the killer—who might just be a werewolf—Hazuki learns that there is much more to their monitored communications than meets the eye.

THE STORIES OF IBIS BY HIROSHI YAMAMOTO

In a world where humans are a minority and androids have created their own civilization, a wandering storyteller meets the beautiful android Ibis. She tells him seven stories of human/android interaction in order to reveal the secret behind humanity's fall. The stories that Ibis speaks of are the "seven novels" about the events surrounding the announcements of the development of artificial intelligence in the twentieth and twenty-first centuries. At a glance, these stories do not appear to have any sort of connection, but what is the true meaning behind them? What are Ibis's real intentions?

ALSO BY HIROSHI SAKURAZAKA:

ALL YOU NEED IS KILL

When the alien Mimics invade, Keiji Kiriya is just one of many recruits shoved into a suit of battle armor called a Jacket and sent out to kill. Keiji dies on the battlefield, only to be reborn each morning to fight and die again and again. On his 158th iteration, he gets a message from a mysterious ally—the female soldier known as the Full Metal Bitch. Is she the key to Keiji's escape or his final death?

VISIT US AT WWW.HAIKASORU.COM